PRAISE FOR *T*
AND GEORG

"The author has pulled off the tour de force of presenting, entirely convincingly, the private thoughts of a great public figure."

—*NEW YORK TIMES*

"The secret vice beneath the outer virtue, the scandalous dream inside the respectable head, the sudden crack in the stucco of propriety—these are the things that interest him to the point of obsession.... It is impossible not to admire the accuracy, the unfailing psychological insight, the unfaltering eye for the small but convincing human details that he brings to his stories of men obsessed. He has been called a master of abnormal psychology. But what makes him really remarkable is a grasp of the fact that the step from the normal to the abnormal—the step beyond the limit—can be frighteningly short in an ordinary life."   —*LIFE*

"Simenon's prose rejoices in the virtues of his virtuosity: it is economical, supple, precise.... But he writes entertainingly about corruption, cruelty or grief because he jousts at human follies without judging them."   —*TIME*

"An intensive, poignant story remarkable for its insight into human worth and human frailty."

—THE BOOK-OF-THE-MONTH CLUB

"I love to read Simenon. He reminds me of Chekhov."

—WILLIAM FAULKNER

"If I hadn't read *Ticket of Leave* (*La Veuve Couderc*), I couldn't have written *The Stranger*." —ALBERT CAMUS

"When they come to me to ask, 'What should I read of his?' I reply, 'Everything.'" —ANDRE GIDE

"He was a writer as comfortable with reality as with fiction, with passion as with reason. Above all, he inspired the confidence that readers reserve for novelists whom they venerate." —JOHN LE CARRÉ

"Few writers are able to express this everyday, intimate, universal realm of thought and sensation [as you]. It makes me envious ... It's what you leave out that makes your books so full of reverberations. You create a real and honest collaboration with your readers." —HENRY MILLER, IN A LETTER TO SIMENON

"Simenon is an all-round master craftsman—ironic, disciplined, highly intelligent, with fine descriptive power. His themes are timeless in their preoccupation with the interrelation of evil, guilt and good; contemporary in their fidelity to the modern context and Gallic in precision, logic and a certain emanation of pain or disquiet. His fluency is of course astonishing." —FRANCIS STEEGMULLER

"There is nothing like winter in the company of a keg of brandy and the complete works of Simenon." —LUIS SEPULVEDA

THE PRESIDENT

GEORGES SIMENON (1903–1989) was born in Liège, Belgium, the son of an accountant. His father's ill health forced him to quit school at 16, and he became a newspaperman, assigned to the crime beat. He published his first book, *Au Point des arches,* a year later, under his reporter's pen-name, G. Sim. In 1922 he moved to Paris and began to write novels at a furious pace, using at least a dozen pen-names, although he created his most famous character, Commissaire Maigret of the Paris Police, under his own name. Maigret would eventually star in 75 novels. His non-Maigret novels—referred to as his *roman durs* (literally, "hard novels")—were even more critically acclaimed, leading to speculation he would eventually win the Nobel. In the early thirties Simenon took up travel, living on a houseboat cruising the Belgian canal system, touring Africa and the Soviet Union, and living throughout the US and Canada. During the war years he moved to the French countryside, but was harassed by the Nazis who suspected his last name was Jewish. Nonetheless, after the war he was banned from publishing for five years for having sold film rights to German filmmakers. Married and divorced twice, Simenon was the father of four children, one of whom, his daughter Mari-Jo, committed suicide at age 25. (She would be the subject of his novel, *The Disappearance of Odile.*) It would darken Simenon's later years, but he never stopped writing. Estimates are that he wrote as many as 500 books by the time of his death of natural causes at age 86.

DAPHNE WOODWARD was also known for her translations from the French of eight novels in Simenon's Inspector Maigret series, as well as the work of Nobel Prize-winner J. M. G. Le Clezio.

THE NEVERSINK LIBRARY

I was by no means the only reader of books on board the Neversink. Several other sailors were diligent readers, though their studies did not lie in the way of belles-lettres. Their favourite authors were such as you may find at the book-stalls around Fulton Market; they were slightly physiological in their nature. My book experiences on board of the frigate proved an example of a fact which every booklover must have experienced before me, namely, that though public libraries have an imposing air, and doubtless contain invaluable volumes, yet, somehow, the books that prove most agreeable, grateful, and companionable, are those we pick up by chance here and there; those which seem put into our hands by Providence; those which pretend to little, but abound in much. —HERMAN MELVILLE, *WHITE JACKET*

THE PRESIDENT

GEORGES SIMENON

TRANSLATED BY DAPHNE WOODWARD

MELVILLE HOUSE PUBLISHING
BROOKLYN, NEW YORK

THE PRESIDENT

Originally published in French as *Le President*

The President © 1958 Georges Simenon Limited, a Chorion company.

Translated by Daphne Woodward
Translation © Penguin Books, Ltd.

Design by Christopher King

First Melville House printing: September 2011

Melville House Publishing
145 Plymouth Street
Brooklyn, NY 11201

www.mhpbooks.com

ISBN: 978-1-935554-62-2

Printed in the United States of America
1 2 3 4 5 6 7 8 9 10

        Library of Congress Cataloging-in-Publication Data

Simenon, Georges, 1903-1989.
 [Président. English]
The president / Georges Simenon.
    p. cm.
ISBN 978-1-935554-62-2
I. Title.
PQ2637.I53P7313 2011
843'.912--dc23

                        2011026233

THE PRESIDENT

CHAPTER 1

FOR MORE THAN AN HOUR HE HAD BEEN SITTING motionless in the old Louis-Philippe armchair, with its almost upright back and shabby black leather upholstery, that he had lugged around with him from one Ministry to another for forty years, till it had become a legend.

They always thought he was asleep when he sat like that with eyelids lowered, raising just one of them from time to time, to reveal a slit of gleaming eyeball. Not only was he not asleep, but he knew exactly what he looked like, his body rather stiff in a black coat that hung loosely on him, something like a frock coat, and his chin resting on the tall, stiff collar that was seen in all his photographs and which he wore like a uniform from the moment he emerged from his bedroom in the morning.

As the years went by his skin had grown thinner and smoother, with white blotches that gave it the appearance of marble, and by now it clung to the prominent cheekbones and sheathed his skeleton so closely that his features, as they became more strongly marked, seemed to be gradually fining down. In the village once he had heard one little boy call out to another:

"Look at that old death's-head!"

He sat without stirring, scarcely a yard away from the log fire, whose flames crackled now and then in a sudden

downdraft, his hands folded on his stomach in the position in which they would be placed when his dead body
was laid out. Would anybody have the nerve, then, to slip a
rosary between his fingers, as someone had done to one of
his colleagues, who'd also been several times Premier and a
leading Freemason?

He had got more and more into the habit of withdraw-
ing like this into immobility and silence, at all times of day,
but most often at dusk, when Mademoiselle Milleran, his
secretary, had come in noiselessly, without stirring the air,
to switch on his parchment-shaded desk lamp, and gone
away again into the next room; and it was as though he'd
erected a wall around himself, or rather as though he had
huddled up tightly into a blanket, retiring from everything
except the sense of his individual existence.

Did he sometimes fall into a doze? If so he wouldn't admit it, convinced that his mind was ceaselessly alert; and to
prove this to himself and to those around him, he would
sometimes amuse himself by describing their comings
and goings.

This afternoon, for instance, Mademoiselle Milleran—
her name was the same, but for one letter, as that of a former
colleague who had been President of the Republic, though
not, it was true, for long—this afternoon, Mademoiselle
Milleran had come in twice on tiptoe and the second time,
after making sure that he wasn't dead, that his chest was still
rising and falling as he breathed, she had pushed back a log
that threaten, to roll out onto the carpet.

He had chosen for himself, as his own corner, the
room nearest to his bedroom, and the massive, unstained,
unpolished wooden table was as plain as a butcher's
chopping block.

This was his famous study, so often photographed that it, too, now belonged to the legend, like every nook and corner of Les Ebergues. The whole world knew that his bedroom was like a monk's cell, that the walls were whitewashed, and that the Premier slept on an iron bedstead.

The public was familiar with every angle of the four low-ceilinged rooms, converted stables or cowsheds, whose interior doors had been removed and whose walls were entirely lined with pitch-pine shelves packed with books.

What was Milleran doing, while he kept his eyes shut? He hadn't dictated anything to her. She had no letters to answer. She didn't knit, didn't sew. And the morning was her time for looking through the newspapers and marking with red pencil any articles that might interest him.

He was convinced that she made notes, rather in the way certain animals heap up in their lair anything and everything they come across, and that once he was dead she'd write her memoirs. He had often tried to catch her at it, but never succeeded. He'd been no more successful when he tried to tease an admission out of her.

One would have sworn that in the next room she was keeping as still as he and that they were spying on each other.

Would she remember the five o'clock news?

Ever since morning a gale had been blowing, threatening to carry away the slates on the roof and the west wall, rattling the windows so that you would have thought someone was continually knocking on them. The Newhaven-Dieppe steamer, after a difficult crossing that had been mentioned on the radio, had had to make three shots at getting into Dieppe harbor, after being almost forced to turn back.

The Premier had insisted on going out, all the same, about eleven o'clock, muffled in his ancient astrakhan coat that had been through so many international conferences, from London to Warsaw, from the Kremlin to Ottawa.

"You surely don't mean to go out?" Madame Blanche, his nurse, had protested on finding him dressed up like that.

She knew that if he wanted to she wouldn't be able to stop him, but she put up a fight in the forlorn hope.

"Dr. Gaffé told you again only yesterday evening . . . "

"Is it the doctor's life or mine that's involved here?"

"Listen, sir . . . At least let me call up the doctor and ask him . . . "

He had merely looked at her with his light-gray eyes, his steely eyes as the newspapers called them. She always began by trying to stare him out, and at such moments anybody would have felt certain they hated each other.

Perhaps, after putting up with her for twelve years, he really had come to hate her? He'd sometimes asked himself. He wasn't sure of the answer. Wasn't she, perhaps, the only person who wasn't awed by his fame? Or who pretended not to be?

In the old days he'd have settled the question without hesitation, confident of his judgment, but as he grew older he was becoming more cautious.

In any case, this woman, who was neither young nor attractive, had ended by absorbing more of his attention than he gave to so-called serious problems. Twice, in a moment of anger, he had thrown her out of Les Ebergues and forbidden her to come back. As it was he wouldn't let her sleep there, although there was a spare room; he made her take lodgings in a house in the village.

Both times she had turned up next morning, in time for his injection, her hard, commonplace, fifty-year-old face entirely devoid of expression.

He hadn't even chosen her. The last time he had been Premier, ten years ago, he'd found her at his side one night when, after speaking for three hours in the Chamber of Deputies in the teeth of relentless opposition, he'd fainted away.

He could still remember his astonishment at finding himself lying on a dusty floor and seeing the white-overalled woman with a hypodermic syringe in her hand, the only serene, comforting face amid the general anxiety.

For some time after that she had come every day to give him treatment at the Hôtel Matignon; and later, when the government fell, to his bachelor flat on the Quai Malaquais.

Les Ebergues had then been still just a country hide-out, bought at haphazard as a place for brief holidays. When he had decided to retire and live there permanently, she had announced, without consulting him:

"I shall come with you."

"And suppose I don't need a nurse?"

"They won't let you go away there without someone to look after you."

"Who are *they*?"

"Professor Fumet, to begin with."

He had been his doctor and friend for more than thirty years.

"*Those gentlemen...*"

He had understood, and the expression had amused him. He still used it to refer to the few dozen people—were there as many as that?—who really ran the country.

"Those gentlemen" didn't mean only the Premier and the Cabinet, the Council of State, the Bench, the Bank of France, and a few senior permanent civil servants, but also applied to the Sûreté Générale, in the Rue des Saussaies, which was concerned that no ill should befall the famous statesman.

Had not two detectives been sent to Bénouville, the
village nearest to Les Ebergues, where they had taken up
residence at the inn so as to mount guard over him, while a
third, who lived at Le Havre with his wife and family, came
on his motorcycle at intervals to take his turn of duty?

At this very moment, despite the squalls and rainbursts
that seemed to come from sea and sky at the same time, one
of the three would be standing leaning against the wet trunk
of the tree by the side gate, with eyes fixed on the lighted
window.

Madame Blanche had come to Bénouville. For a long
time he had supposed she was a widow, or that, although
a spinster, she, like many old maids in jobs, had herself addressed as "Madame" to enhance her dignity.

It was three years before he discovered that she had a
husband in Paris, a certain Louis Blain, who kept a book-
shop near Saint-Sulpice, specializing in religious works. She
had never mentioned it to him, she simply went up to Paris
once a month.

One day when he was in a bad temper he had growled,
while she was attending to him with her usual calm face:

"You must admit you're a stiff-necked woman! I might
almost say a depraved woman, in one sense of the word.
There you are, fresh as if you'd just got up, not a hair out of
place, mind and body alert, and you come into the bedroom
of an old man who's gradually rotting away. Incidentally,
does my room stink in the morning?"

"It smells like any other bedroom."

"Before I grew old myself I used to be sickened by the
smell of old men. But you, you pretend not to notice. You
have the satisfaction of saying to yourself:

"'The man I see every morning, ugly and naked, half

dead already, is the same one whose name is in all the history books, and who any day now will have his statue, or at least his avenue, in most of the towns of France. . . .' Like Gambetta! . . . Like poor Jaurés, whom I knew so well. . . . "

She had merely inquired:

"Are you keen on your name being given to avenues?"

Perhaps it was precisely because she saw him naked, a weak old man, that he resented her?

And yet he didn't resent Emile, his chauffeur and valet, who was equally familiar with his sordid, unadorned privacy.

Was that because Emile was a man?

Anyhow, Madame Blanche and Emile had gone out with him, into the north wind that forced them to bend double, Madame Blanche with her cape, which flapped like a loose sail. Emile in his strict, black uniform with the tight-fitting leather gaiters.

There were no excursionists to photograph them that morning, and no journalists, nobody except Soulas, the swarthiest of the three detectives, smoking a damp cigarette beneath his tree and beating his arms across his chest now and then to warm himself.

The house, which had no upper story except for three little attic rooms above the kitchen, consisted of two buildings that had been connected together, and stood all alone, or rather crouched on the cliff-top, about a quarter of a mile from the village of Bénouville, between Etretat and Fécamp.

As usual, Emile walked on the Premier's left, ready to prop him up if his leg gave way, and Madame Blanche, obeying the orders he had given her once and for all, followed a few paces behind.

This daily walk had also been publicized by the press,

and in summer a tourist agency at Fécamp would bring bus-loads of excursionists to watch from a distance.

A narrow lane, starting from behind the house, wound through the fields till it joined the coast-guard path, at the very edge of the cliff. The land belonged to a local farmer who turned his cows out to graze there, and from time to time the ground would crumble beneath the hoofs of one of the beasts, which would be found three hundred feet below, on the rocks of the shore.

He knew he was wrong to go out in bad weather. All his life he had known when he was wrong, but all his life he had persisted, as though challenging fate. Had he done so badly, after all?

The drifting sky was low. One saw it moving in from the open sea, bringing dark clouds that broke into tatters, and the air tasted of salt and seaweed; the same wind that was whipping up evil-looking white horses on the surface of the water was storming the cliffs to fling itself savagely on the countryside.

Through the roar he heard Madame Blanche's voice coming faintly from behind:

"Sir ... "

No! He had made up his mind to go to the edge, to watch the wild sea, before going back to be an invalid in the Louis-Philippe armchair.

He was being careful about his leg. He knew it well, better than Gaffé, the young doctor from Le Havre who came every day to see him, better than Lalinde, the former staff doctor, who paid a "friendly visit" from Rouen once a week, better even than. Professor Fumet, who was only sent for on serious occasions.

It might happen any moment. Since the attack three

years ago, that had kept him in bed for nine weeks, and then on a chaise-longue, his way of walking had never been quite natural. His left leg seemed to float, as it were. It seemed to take its time about obeying, and whenever it moved forward there was a slight sideways motion, at each step, that he couldn't prevent.

"I waddle like a duck!" he had said jokingly at the time. Nobody had laughed. He'd been the only one who'd made light of the business. And yet he followed, with almost impassioned interest, everything that went on inside him.

It had begun one morning when he was out for his walk, just like today except that in those days he used to go farther, as far as the dip in the cliffs which was known as the Valleuse du Curé.

He'd never had a moment's anxiety except about his heart, which had played him a few tricks, and he'd been advised to take care of it. It had never occurred to him that his legs, let alone his hands, might let him down as well.

That day—it was in March; the weather was bright and cold; the white cliffs of England had been visible in the distance—he had felt in his left leg, beginning at the thigh and creeping slowly downwards, a skin-deep warmth accompanied by the prickly sensation that one feels, for instance, after sitting for a long time beside a stove or in front of a log fire.

With no uneasiness, curious as to what was happening to him, he had gone on walking, his faithful stick in his hand (his pilgrim's staff, as the papers called it), until, without thinking, he had rubbed his thigh with his hand. To his stupefaction, it had been rather like touching another person's body. There was no contact. He was touching his own flesh, pinching it, and he felt it no more than if his flesh had been cardboard.

Had that scared him? He had turned around to tell Madame Blanche about it when, all of a sudden, his leg had given way, slipped from under him, and he had found himself huddled up at the side of the path.

He felt no pain, had no sense of any danger, was simply conscious of his ridiculous posture and the rotten trick his leg had so unexpectedly played him.

"Help me up, Emile!" he had said, stretching out his hand.

In the Chamber of Deputies, where everyone, or almost everyone, uses "*tu*" and affects Christian-name terms with everyone else, he had never addressed anyone in that way; nor did he even use "*tu*" to his cook-housekeeper, Gabrielle, who had been with him for more than forty years. He called his secretary by her surname, Milleran, as if she were a man, without ever using "*tu,*" and Madame Blanche was always Madame Blanche as far as he was concerned.

"You didn't hurt yourself?"

He had noticed that the nurse, bending over him, had turned pale, for the first time in his acquaintance with her, but he hadn't attributed any importance to it.

"Don't get up for a moment," she had advised. "Tell me first of all whether ... "

He was struggling to stand up, with Emile's help, and then his eyes had, despite himself, become a little set, his voice had been slightly less assured than usual, as he observed:

"Funny thing ... It won't take my weight any more... "
He had lost his left leg. It wasn't his, any longer. It refused to obey him!

"Help him to sit down, Emile. You'll have to go and fetch ... "

She must have known, just as the others knew later on. Fumet, who understood his character, had offered to tell him frankly what had happened. He'd said no. He refused to be ill. He didn't want to know his illness, and not for a moment had he been tempted to open one of his medical books.

"Can you carry me, Emile?"

"Certainly, sir."

Madame Blanche protested. He didn't give in. It was impossible to bring the car along that narrow path. They'd have to fetch a stretcher, probably from the priest, who doubtless kept one in reserve for burials.

He preferred to cling with his arms around the neck of Emile, who was strongly built and had firm muscles.

"If you get tired, put me down in the grass for a bit...."

"It'll be all right."

Gabrielle watched them coming, standing in the door of her kitchen. This was before he'd taken on young Marie to help her.

Less than half an hour later, Dr. Gaffé, who must have driven like a lunatic, was by his bedside, and almost at once he rang up Dr. Lalinde at Rouen.

It wasn't till about four o'clock that, glancing at his hand, the Premier noticed it looked funny. He moved his fingers playfully, like a child, and these fingers didn't take their usual positions.

"Look at this, Doctor!"

It hadn't surprised Gaffé, who had not gone home to Le Havre for lunch, nor Lalinde, who had arrived about two o'clock and had afterwards made a long telephone call to Paris.

Later on, he learned that for several days one of his eyes had been fixed, his mouth twisted.

"A stroke, I suppose?"

He could hardly speak. They hadn't answered him, one way or the other, but the professor had arrived that same evening, followed by an ambulance which, a little later, took the lot of them off to Rouen.

"I give you my word, my dear Premier," Fumet said, "that you won't be kept in the clinic against your will. It's not a matter of getting you into hospital, only of taking X rays and making tests that aren't possible here...."

Contrary to his expectation, it wasn't an unpleasant memory. He remained very detached. He watched them all: Gaffé, who hadn't begun to breathe more freely until Lalinde had arrived to share his responsibility; Lalinde himself, sandy-haired, rosy-cheeked, blue-eyed, with bushy eyebrows, trying to give an impression of self-confidence; then Fumet, the big man, used to distinguished patients and to the little court of admiring disciples that followed him from bed to bed as he made his rounds.

When they felt obliged to withdraw into corners to talk in low tones, he amused himself by studying the characters of the three men, and the idea of death didn't even occur to him.

He'd been seventy-eight years old at that time. The first question he had asked at Rouen, while he was being undressed and the X-ray apparatus was got ready, was:

"Did the inspectors come along behind?"

Nobody had paid attention, but they were surely there, or one of them at least, and the alarm had certainly been given to the Ministry of the Interior.

There had been some unpleasant moments, particularly when he'd been given a lumbar puncture and again when they'd taken an encephalogram. But he had never stopped joking, and at about four in the morning, when they were busy in the laboratory, he asked whether someone could get him a quarter bottle of champagne.

The funny thing was that they'd found him one, in a rather shady Rouen night club that was still open, and probably it was one of the policemen, one of his watchdogs, as he sometimes called them, who had been sent on the errand.

That was a long time ago, now. It was no more than a story to tell. For two months the village of Bénouville had been invaded by French and foreign journalists determined to be in at his death. In the newspaper offices the obituary notices had been written, blocks made of photographs with some claim to be historic, and the printers stood by ready to set it all up.

Wouldn't the same articles be used sooner or later, with a change of date and a few details, for he had taken no part in politics since then?

He'd never fallen again, like a tripped hare, but now and then, though less acutely, he'd had the feeling that his leg was taking its time to obey him. It sometimes came over him at night, too, in bed, a sort of cramp, or rather, a numbness that didn't hurt at all. When it happened out walking, Emile would notice almost at the same time as himself. A kind of signal passed between them. Emile would come closer and the Premier would clutch his shoulder, stand still, though without taking his eyes off the landscape. Madame Blanche would come up then, and hand him a pink tablet, which he would swallow without a word.

The three of them would wait in silence. It had happened once in the middle of the village, when people were just coming out of mass, and the peasants had wondered why they stood riveted to the ground like that, for the Premier didn't appear to be in pain, or out of breath, and he made it a point of vanity to keep smiling vaguely all the time.

He hated it to happen on days when Madame Blanche had urged him not to go out, and so this morning he'd paid more attention than usual to the behavior of his leg. For fear of putting the nurse in the right, he had not stayed out long; all the same, he had sneezed twice.

When they got back he had flung at her triumphantly:

"You see!"

"Wait till tomorrow to find out if you've not caught a cold."

That was her way. One had to take her as she was. Whereas Milleran, the secretary, never resisted him, was so unobtrusive that he hardly noticed her presence in the house. She was pale, with soft, blurred features, and anybody who had only seen her two or three times would probably not have recognized her again. All the same she was efficient, and at this moment, for example, he felt sure she had her eye on the little clock in her office, waiting to come in on the dot and turn on his radio.

The ministerial crisis had lasted a week, and as usual the Republic was said to be in danger. Cournot, the French President, had sent for about a dozen political leaders in succession, and didn't know where to turn next.

He'd known Cournot as a very young man, fresh from Montauban, where his father sold bicycles. He was a militant Socialist, one of those who sit in gloomy offices, dealing with tiresome secretarial work, and are seldom heard of except at annual conferences. He hardly ever spoke in the Chamber, and when he did it was usually at night sittings, to almost empty benches.

Had Cournot realized, when he chose that self-effacing

line, that it would lead him one day to the Elysée, where his two daughters, with their husbands and children, had moved in at the same time as he did?

One eyelid slightly raised, his hands still folded on his stomach, sitting stiff-backed in the Louis-Philippe arm-chair, he was watching the clock, like his secretary next door; but his clock, presented to him by the President of the United States during a state visit to Washington, was a historic piece, which would end up in some museum.

Unless Les Ebergues were itself to become a museum, as some people were already suggesting, and everything should stay in its place, with Emile as custodian.

He felt sure Emile had been thinking about it for several years, the way another man might think of his pension. Wasn't time beginning to drag for him, as he looked forward to the little speech he would make to visitors, to the tips they would slip into his hand on leaving, and the souvenir postcards he might perhaps sell?

At two minutes to five, fearing Milleran might be the first to move, he put out his hand noiselessly, furtively, and turned the knob on the radio set. The dial lit up, but for a few seconds no sound came. In the next room, for there was no door between it and the Premier's study, the secretary got to her feet and at the very moment when she came tiptoeing in, music blared out, a jazz tune in which the trumpets seemed to be challenging the noise of the storm.

"I'm sorry ... " she murmured.

"You see, I wasn't asleep!"

"I know."

Madame Blanche, in such circumstances, would have smiled, sarcastically or disbelievingly. Milleran simply vanished as though she had melted into thin air.

"At the third pip it will be precisely ... "

It was too early yet for the proper news bulletin, which would be broadcast at a quarter past seven, but there was a short summary of the latest headlines, between two musical programs:

"This is Paris-Inter calling... After devoting last night and this morning to consultations, Monsieur François Bourdieu, Leader of the Socialist Group, was received by the President of the Republic at three o'clock this afternoon and informed him that he was giving up his attempt to form a Cabinet...."

The Premier's face betrayed no sign of his feelings, as he still sat motionless in his armchair, but his fingers were clenched now and the tips had gone whiter.

The announcer had a cold and coughed twice over the microphone. There came a rustle of papers, then:

"According to unconfirmed rumors circulating in the corridors of the Chamber, Monsieur Cournot is said to have requested Monsieur Philippe Chalamont, Leader of the Left Independent Group, to visit him late this afternoon, and to be intending to ask him to form a coalition government.... Argentina... The general strike which was called yesterday at Buenos Aires, and which had brought out about seventy per cent of workers ... "

The voice broke off without warning in the middle of a sentence; at the same time the lights in the study and the neighboring rooms went out, and now there was nothing except the sound of the wind, the dancing firelight.

He didn't move. Milleran, next door, struck a match, opened the drawer where she kept a supply of candles, for it was not the first time this had happened.

There was a brief flash as the lights seemed to be coming on again, the bulbs gave out a cloudy glow, like those of certain night trains, then they faded slowly and it was complete darkness.

"I'll bring you a candle at once...."

Before she had had time to stick it upright on a china ashtray, a light appeared, moving along a passage that connected the former cowsheds with the kitchen and the rest of the house. This passage, which had not existed in the old days and which the Premier had had built, was known as the tunnel.

It was Gabrielle, the old cook, who was coming through the tunnel now, brandishing a big oil lamp with pink flowers painted on its globe.

"The young doctor has just arrived, sir," announced Gabrielle; she always referred thus to Dr. Gaffé, who was just thirty-two, to distinguish him from Dr. Lalinde.

"Where is he?"

"In the kitchen, with Madame Blanche."

This made him suddenly angry, perhaps because of the name that had been mentioned on the radio and the news that had been broadcast.

"Why did he come in by the kitchen?"

"Well now, I never asked him!"

"What are they doing?"

"They're having a chat, while the doctor warms his hands at my stove. After all, he can't touch you with icy-cold hands."

He loathed not being informed of comings and goings in the house.

"I've told you a hundred times ..."

"I know, I know! It's not me you ought to tell. It's the people that come; I can't shut the door of my kitchen in their faces."

There was a front door by which Milleran was supposed

to let in visitors. It was perfectly visible, being lit by a lantern. But more often than not people would persist in coming in through the kitchen, whence a murmur of unknown voices would suddenly become audible.

"Tell the doctor I'm waiting."

Then he called:

"Milleran!"

"Yes, sir."

"Is the telephone working?"

She tried it.

"Yes, I can hear the click."

"Ask the electric company how long it will take them to repair . . . "

"Very good, sir . . . "

He received Dr. Gaffé in a cold, unsmiling silence which made the doctor, who was shy by nature, feel more awkward than ever.

"Madame Blanche tells me you went for a walk this morning?"

The young doctor made this remark in a casual tone while opening his bag, and he received no answer.

"In weather like this," the doctor went on, embarrassed, "it was perhaps a little unwise . . . "

Madame Blanche came forward to help the Premier out of his coat. He stopped her with a glance, took it off himself, rolled up his shirt sleeve. Milleran's voice could be heard on the telephone, then she came in to announce:

"They don't know yet. There's been a general breakdown. They think it's the cable that . . . "

"Leave us."

Dr. Gaffé came to see him every day at the same time, and nearly every day he solemnly took his blood pressure.

The Premier had asked him once:

"You think it's necessary?"

"It's an excellent precaution."

"You make a point of it?"

Gaffé had got flustered. At his age he still blushed. He was so much in awe of his patient that once when he had to give him an injection he had fumbled so badly that Madame Blanche had been obliged to take the hypodermic away from him.

"You make a point of it?" the Premier had insisted. "Well, the thing is . . . "

"Is what?"

"I think Professor Fumet makes a point of it."

"It's he who gives you instructions?"

"Of course."

"And he alone?"

What was the use of forcing the doctor to tell a lie? Fumet himself must have had orders from higher quarters. Because the Premier, while still alive, had become a historical personage, he wasn't allowed to take care of his health just as he thought fit. They pretended to obey him, the whole pack of them, but who gave them their real orders? And to whom, God knows when, God knows how, did they report?

Was it also by order that visitors went to the kitchen instead of ringing at the front door?

Gabrielle had told the truth: Gaffé's hands were still cold and the Premier thought he looked ridiculous, squeezing the little rubber bulb and staring very solemnly at the needle on the round dial.

Because he was cross, he deliberately refrained from asking, as he usually did, out of politeness as it were:

"How much?"

Nonetheless, Gaffé murmured, his satisfaction no less absurd than his solemnity:

"Seventeen...."

The same as the day before, the day before that, every day for months and months past!

"Any pain, any discomfort during the night?"

"Nothing."

"And your leg?"

He was feeling his pulse and the Premier couldn't restrain himself from glaring resentfully at him.

"No respiratory difficulty?"

"No respiratory difficulty," he replied curtly, "and I may as well tell you at once that I made water in the usual way."

For he knew that would be the next question.

"I wonder if this electric failure ... " muttered Gaffé.

Without listening to him, the Premier was putting on his coat, with the same sour expression, taking care to avoid Madame Blanche's eye, for he did not want to lose his temper.

Probably because of the electric failure, the consequent silence of the radio which was his only contact with the outside world, he felt like a prisoner in this cottage flattened on the cliff-top, between the black hole of the sea and the black countryside which was not even dotted any longer with the little twinkling lights that indicated the presence of life.

The oil lamp in his study, the candle in Milleran's office, its flame wavering with each draft, reminded him of the stickiest evenings in his childhood, when the houses didn't yet have electric light and gas had not been brought to Evreux.

Hadn't Gaffé said something just now about respiratory

difficulties? He might have answered that he suddenly felt as though he were being physically and morally smothered.

He had been shut up at Les Ebergues and the few human beings who surrounded him had become his jailers, whether they wanted to or not.

He was forgetting that it was he who had left Paris, swearing dramatically that he would never set foot there again, in a sulky mood, because ... But that was another story. His reasons were his own business, and everybody, papers and politicians alike, had misinterpreted his retirement.

Was it he who insisted that this young doctor, a nice young fellow, but a silly greenhorn, should come every day from Le Havre to take his blood pressure and ask him some footling questions, always the same ones? Was it he who was forcing two poor devils of police inspectors to live at the inn at Bénouville, and a third to settle at Le Havre with his wife and children, so as to mount guard under the elm beside the gate?

All right, so he was in a bad temper. These fits of anger had come over him all his life, just as some people feel the blood running to their heads, or some women grow suddenly depressed. For forty years his rages had been the terror not only of his own staff but of many people in high places, including generals, leading magistrates, statesmen.

The effect on him was the same as that produced on other people by alcohol, which doesn't always cloud the intelligence but sometimes stimulates it, and his bouts of ill-temper didn't throw him off his course. Far from it!

The electric failure was going to last, he knew it was. He didn't go so far as to suggest that they had engineered it on purpose, though that would have been perfectly possible.

"I'll be here tomorrow at the same time, Premier ..."

faltered the doctor, whom Madame Blanche was about to escort through the tunnel again.

"Not that way!" he protested. "By the proper door, please."

"I beg your pardon. . . . "

"Not at all."

It was he who went to the tunnel, and called out:

"Emile!"

"Yes, sir."

"Bring the car under the window and fix it like last time. You can manage it?"

"Certainly."

"Get it going by seven o'clock, if the lights haven't come on again."

"I'll see to it at once."

At that moment the telephone rang. Milleran's flat voice could be heard saying:

"Les Ebergues, yes . . . Who is speaking? . . . A call from the Elysée? . . . Just a moment, please. . . . Hold on. . . . "

He suspected nothing, let himself be caught, as on previous occasions.

"Hello?"

As soon as he heard the voice he understood, but all the same he listened to the end.

"That you, Augustin?"

A pause, as usual.

"Xavier here. . . . You'd better hurry, old chap. . . . Don't forget I've promised to be at your funeral, and here I am in hospital again. . . . "

A whinnying laugh. Silence. At last, a click.

Milleran had understood.

"I beg your pardon," she stuttered, taking the blame on herself and fading into the semidarkness of her office.

CHAPTER 2

HE HAD A BOOK ON HIS KNEES, THE *MEMOIRES de Sully*, but he was not turning the pages, and Milleran, her ear cocked in the next room, was about to come in and make sure the oil lamp was giving him enough light, when he spoke to her. He would sometimes keep silent for two hours and then give her an order or ask her a question as though she'd been sitting in front of him, and he felt so sure of her that he would not have forgiven any lapse in her attention.

"Ask the post office where that call came from."

"I'll do it at once, sir."

Still staring at the page of his book, he heard her at the telephone, and she soon informed him, without leaving her chair:

"Evreux."

"Thank you."

He had suspected as much. Yet Xavier Malate's last call, two months earlier, had come from Strasbourg; the previous one, much further back, from the Hopital Cochin in Paris.

In the whole course of his life the Premier had avoided forming an attachment to anybody, not so much from principle, or from hardheartedness, as to safeguard his independence, which he prized above all else. The only woman he ever married came into his life for a brief three years, long enough to bear him one daughter, and that daughter, now a woman of forty-five, married, with a son in his first year of Law School, had always been a stranger to him.

He was eighty-two years old. All he wanted now was peace, and that he thought he had attained. Strangely enough, the only human being who still clung to him and had the power, at a distance, to disturb him so much that he couldn't read, was a man for whom he cared nothing, now or at any other time.

Was this Malate's importance due to the fact that of all the members of his own generation with whom he had had any degree of intimacy, he was the sole survivor?

Malate used to declare confidently, as though announcing a certainty:

"I'll be at your funeral."

He himself had been in hospital a dozen times, in Paris and elsewhere. A dozen times the doctors had given him only a few weeks to live. Each time he'd bounced up again, returned to the surface, and he was still there, with his obsession about outliving his old schoolfellow.

A long time ago somebody had said:

"He's a harmless imbecile."

The speaker, whoever he was, had been astonished by the reaction of the Premier, whose cordiality had suddenly vanished as he answered curtly, as though touched on the raw:

"There is no such thing as a harmless imbecile."

After a pause he had added, as though he had been wondering whether to speak his mind to the full:

"There is no such thing as an imbecile."

He had proffered no further explanation. It was difficult

to put into words. Underlying a certain kind of stupidity, he suspected something Machiavellian that frightened him. He refused to believe it could be unconscious.

By what right had Xavier Malate irrupted into his life and stubbornly kept his place there? What feelings or thought processes prompted him to the tricks, never twice the same, that brought his boyhood friend to the telephone to listen to the mean message he delivered in his harsh voice?

The Premier knew the hospital, in the Rue Saint-Louis at Evreux, from which this latest call had been made. It was only a few yards from the house where Malate's father had had his printing works, at the corner of the next street, to be precise.

He and Xavier had been at the town *lycée*, in the same form; and it must have been in the third form, when they were both a little over thirteen years old, that the thing had happened.

Later on, Malate had claimed that it was the future Cabinet Minister and Premier who had had the original idea. That was possible, but by no means certain, for the Premier himself could not remember making the suggestion, which didn't seem like him.

All the same, he had joined in the conspiracy. At that time they had an English master whose name he had now forgotten, like those of at least half his schoolmates, in spite of the important part the man had played in his life for four years.

He could still see him pretty clearly, however, short, badly dressed, always wearing a black jacket too big for him and shiny with age, his hair hanging in gray elf-locks under his bowler hat. He reminded one of a priest, especially as he was a bachelor and was perpetually reading a black-bound volume of Shakespeare that looked like a breviary.

He seemed very old to the boys, but he could not have
been more than fifty-five to sixty, and his mother was still
alive; he used to visit her at Rouen from Saturday evening
to Monday morning.

People called him an imbecile too, because he conducted
classes without appearing to see his pupils, for whom he
seemed to feel a lofty contempt, if not a measure of disgust,
and his only reaction if one of them grew restless, was to
give him two hundred lines.

It was too late to find out what he had really been like,
what he used to think.

The practical joke had taken some time to prepare, for
success depended on the most careful planning. With the
help of an old workman employed by his father, Xavier Malate had undertaken the hardest part, the setting up and
printing of about fifty invitations to the teacher's funeral, on
paper with a deep black border.

These had been posted one Saturday evening, for delivery on the Sunday morning, for in those days letters were
still delivered on Sundays. They had made quite sure that
the English master had set out by train for Rouen, whence
he would return at seven minutes past eight on the Monday
morning, in time to drop his bag at home before his first
lesson at nine o'clock.

He lived in a humble street, on the first floor, above one
of those local grocer's shops whose windows display jars
of sweets, tinned foods, a few vegetables, and whose door
rings a bell as it opens.

The funeral invitations had said that the coffin would
be fetched at half past eight, and they had managed, heaven
knows how, to get the hearse used for paupers' burials in
front of the house on the minute.

Some ingenuity had been displayed in selecting the people to whom the invitations were sent: several town councilors, other local authorities, some shopkeepers who supplied the *lycée*, and even the parents of a few younger boys, who were not in the secret.

The conspirators had not been there, since they had a class at eight o'clock. What exactly had happened? The Premier, though he remembered the preparations in some detail, had entirely forgotten what occurred afterwards and could only depend on what Malate had told him, years later.

In any case there had been no English lesson that morning. The master had stayed away for over a week, ill, so they said. The headmaster had opened an inquiry. Malate's guilt had been easily proved, and for several days there had been speculation as to whether he would give away his accomplices.

He had held his tongue, thus becoming a kind of hero. A hero never seen at the *lycée* again, by the way, for in spite of wirepulling by his father, who was the printer of the little local paper, he had been expelled and sent to boarding school at Chartres.

Was it true that he had run away from there, been found by the police at Le Havre, where he was trying to stowaway on board a ship, sent as an apprentice to an uncle who had an import business at Marseilles?

It was perfectly possible, and of no real importance. For the next thirty years, as far as the Premier was concerned, Malate had ceased to exist, like the English master and so many of his other schoolfellows.

He had met him again when he was forty-two years old, a Cabinet Minister for the first time, at the Ministry of Public Works in the Boulevard Saint-Germain.

Every day for a week, at about ten in the morning, the office messenger had brought him a slip bearing the name X. Malate, with the space left for the purpose of visit filled in by the words "Strictly personal," underlined twice.

In his memory the name was vaguely associated with a face, hair that needed cutting, and thin legs, but that was all.

Seven times running he had told the messenger:

"Say I'm at a meeting."

The eighth time he had given way. As a Deputy, he had learned by experience that the only hope of getting rid of a certain type of pest is by seeing them. He remembered an old lady, always dressed in black, with a wheezy dog tucked under her arm, who had haunted various government offices day after day for two years, trying to get her brother into the Académie Française.

Malate had come into the rather austere-looking office, and the thin, knobby-kneed lad had grown to be a tall, fat man with the unhealthy red face of a heavy drinker and bulging eyes. Very much at ease, he held out his hand as though they had seen each other only the day before.

"How are you, Augustin, old boy?"

"Sit down."

"Don't you recognize me?"

"I do."

"Well then?"

His eye had a slightly aggressive glint, which meant, of course:

"So now you're a Minister you cut your old pals?"

At ten o'clock in the morning he already smelled of drink, and though his suit was well tailored it showed traces of the kind of bohemian negligence that the Premier detested.

"Don't be frightened, Augustin. I'm not going to waste

your time. I know it's valuable, and I've not got much to ask you...."

"It's true, I'm extremely busy."

"Heavens! I realize that all right. Since we left Evreux, I first, you'll remember, a lot of time has gone by and we've grown from kids into men. You've done well, and I congratulate you. I've not done so badly either, I'm married, I have two kids, and if I can get just the slightest bit of help, everything will be grand...."

In cases like this the Premier turned to ice, not so much from hardness of heart as from clear-sightedness. He had realized that, whatever one did for him, Xavier Malate would all his life be in need of just a bit more help.

"A contract for enlarging the harbor at Algiers is to be given out next month, and it just so happens that I work in a big engineering concern in which my brother-in-law is a partner...."

A surreptitious touch on the bell warned the messenger, who promptly opened the door.

"Take Monsieur Malate to see Monsieur Beurant."

Malate must have got the wrong idea, for he broke into effusive gratitude:

"Thank you, old man. I knew I could count on you. You realize, don't you, that if it hadn't been for me you'd have been expelled from school too, and then you'd probably not be here now? Ah, well! Honesty is the best policy, whatever they may say. I suppose it's practically in the bag?"

"No."

"What d'you mean?"

"That you must put your case before the head of the contracts department."

"But you'll explain to him that ... "

"I'm going to ring through and ask him to give you ten minutes. That's all."

He had eventually used "*tu*" to him, after all, and regretted it as a weakness, almost a piece of cowardice.

Later on he had received nauseating letters in which talked about his wife, who had twice attempted suicide, and so he daren't leave her alone any more, his children who hadn't enough to eat and couldn't go to school because they had no decent clothes.

He had stopped asking for a government contract, but was pleading for help of any kind, for a job, however humble, even as a lock-keeper or as watchman on road works.

Malate had no suspicion that his former Evreux schoolfellow had asked for his police record from the Rue des Saussaies, and he persisted, his letters growing steadily longer and more tedious, or more harrowing.

He had been inditing such letters, which were nearly all on café notepaper, for over twenty years, sometimes changing his victim, occasionally achieving his aim, and though he had married and was a father, he had deserted his wife and children ten years ago.

"He's here again, sir," the messenger would announce from time to time.

Malate altered his tactics, taking to hanging around the ministerial building, looking seedy and unshaven, in the hope that his one-time schoolmate would take pity on him.

One morning his former friend had walked straight up to him and declared curtly:

"The next time I see you anywhere near here, I'll have you arrested."

In the course of his career he had disappointed other

hopes, had shown himself unrelenting to quite a number of people.

Malate was the only one who had taken a kind of revenge, and the years had not softened his hatred.

He had succeeded up to a point, for on several occasions the Premier had approached the Rue des Saussaies to find out where he was.

"*I'm in hospital at Dakar with a stiff bout of malaria. But you needn't gloat. I shan't peg out this time, because I've sworn I'll be at your funeral.*"

He really was at Dakar. Then in prison at Bordeaux, where he'd been given twelve months for writing rubber checks. From there he had written, on a sheet of prison paper:

"*Life's a funny thing! One man becomes a Cabinet Minister, another becomes a convict.*"

The word "convict" was exaggerated, but dramatic.

"*All the same, I'll be at your funeral.*"

The office of Premier didn't intimidate him, and in fact it was to the Hôtel Matignon that he first began to telephone, giving the name of some politician or celebrity.

"Xavier here . . . Well? How does it feel to be Premier? . . . All the same, you know, I'll still be at your. . . "

The electric lights had not come on again, and Milleran, too, had an oil lamp now. The treacly-looking circles of light in the dusky rooms recalled his old home at Evreux. The Premier even remembered, all of a sudden, the peculiar smell his father's clothes used to have when he got home, for, being the local doctor, an odor of camphor and phenol used to trail around with him. Of red wine, too.

"Call up and find out what's happening about the electricity."

She tried, announced before long:

"The telephone's cut off as well, now."

Gabrielle appeared, to announce:

"Dinner is ready, sir."

"I'm coming at once. . . . "

He didn't feel he was to blame about Malate, and he was only annoyed with himself for allowing his former friend's threat to get on his nerves. He, who believed in nothing except a certain human dignity he could hardly have put into words, in freedom too, at any rate in a measure of freedom of thought, was beginning to suspect Xavier Malate of having baleful powers.

Logically, considering the unhealthy life he had been leading for forty years and more now, the printer's son should have been dead. Not a year went by without his paying a visit, long or short, to some hospital or other. He had even been found to have tuberculosis and sent to a mountain sanatorium where patients died every week, and from which he had emerged cured.

He had had three or four operations, the last two for cancer of the throat, and now, going round and round in imperceptibly diminishing circles, he was back at his starting point, Evreux, as though he had decided to die in his native town.

"Milleran!"

"Yes, sir?"

"Call up the hospital at Evreux tomorrow and ask them to read you the record of a man called Xavier Malate."

It was not the first time she had dealt with the matter, and she asked no questions. Through the window Emile could be heard, bringing the Rolls alongside the house. The black limousine, with its old-fashioned wheels, was more than twenty years old, but like so many other things in this place it belonged, as it were, to the Premier's personality. It had been presented to him by the Lord Mayor of London, on behalf of the citizens of the English capital, when he had been given the Freedom of the City.

Walking slowly, with his hands behind his back, he went along the tunnel to the dining room, with its blackened beams, where a solitary place was laid on a long, narrow table that Came from some former convent or monastery.

Here too the walls were whitewashed, as they are in the poorest villager's cottage, and there was not a single picture or ornament; the floor was paved with the same gray, worn flagstones as the kitchen.

An oil lamp stood in the middle of the table, and it was not Gabrielle who served, but young Marie, taken on two years ago when she was only sixteen.

The first day he had heard her asking Gabrielle:

"What time's the old boy have his dinner?"

He would never be anything more to her than "the old boy." She had heavy breasts, her dress was too tight, and on her weekly day off she made herself up like a tart. Looking out of his window one evening, the Premier had seen her under the elm, her skirts hitched up to her waist, her hands behind her clutching the trunk of the tree, placidly satisfying the needs of one of the policemen. He was doubtless not the only one, and in the overheated rooms she gave off a strong feminine odor.

"Do you think it's proper, sir, for you to have a girl like that here?"

His only answer to Gabrielle's question had been a rather melancholy:

"Why not?"

After all, in earlier days hadn't he occasionally come across Gabrielle in intimate converse with a delivery man, and once with a policeman in uniform?

"I can't understand you. You let her do whatever she likes. She's the only person in the house who's never scolded."

Perhaps that was because he didn't expect her to be faithful or devoted, only to do the heavy work for which he had engaged her. Perhaps, too, because she was eighteen years old, healthy, sturdy, and common, and the last person of that type that he was likely to have about him?

She represented a generation about which he knew nothing, to which he was and would remain just the old boy.

His dinner was always the same, having been prescribed once and for all by Professor Fumet, and Marie had found that astounding, too: a poached egg on dry toast, a glass of milk, a bit of cottage cheese, and some fresh fruit.

He had ceased long ago to feel this as a privation. He even felt surprised, almost disgusted, at the thought that intelligent men, with serious problems to solve every day of their lives, could bother about food and, in the company of pretty women, so much enjoy talking about it.

One day when he had been walking with Emile down a street at Rouen, he had stopped short outside a food shop and gazed for a long time at the trussed fowls, a pheasant *en geleé* still decked with its many-colored tail, a ewe-lamb lying on a bed of fresh, costly greenstuff.

"What do you think of that?"

"They say it's the best shop in Rouen."

He had spoken for his own benefit, not for Emile's:

"Man is the only animal who finds it necessary to decorate the corpses of his victims in order to whet his appetite. Look at those neat rounds of truffle slipped under the skin of the capons to make a symmetrical pattern, that cooked pheasant with his beak and tail so artistically put back in place...."

It was twenty-five years since he had last smoked a cigarette, and only rarely was he allowed a glass of champagne.

He didn't rebel, felt no bitterness. He obeyed his doctors, though not for fear of dying, for death had long since ceased to frighten him. He lived with it in an intimate relationship which, if not cheerful, was at least resigned.

He had been mistaken just now in thinking that he and Xavier Malate were the only survivors of their generation. Unless Eveline had died since his last birthday. She was a sort of counterbalance to the printer's son. His recollection of her was rather vague, although he'd been in love with her when he was about twelve years old.

Her father had kept the ironmonger's shop in the Rue Saint-Louis, nearly opposite the lycée, and she'd been two or three years older than himself, so she would be about eighty-five now.

Had he ever spoken to her? Two or three times, perhaps. He wasn't even sure, at that, that he wasn't mixing her up with sher sister or some other little girl in the district. On the other hand, he was positive that she'd had red hair, fiery red, was thin and lanky, with two pigtails hanging down her back, and wore a pinafore with small red checks.

She had waited before writing to him, not only till he became a Minister but until he was Prime Minister, on the eve of an international conference where the destiny of France was at stake, or so people believed, as they always do. Didn't he believe so himself at the time?

Eveline didn't ask him for anything, but sent him an

envelope containing a little medal from Lourdes, with a note saying:

"*I shall pray that you may succeed in your task. This will help you to save the country.*

"*The little girl from the Rue Saint-Louis—*

"*Eveline ARCHAMBAULT.*"

She had never married, presumably, for Archambault was the name he could see in his mind's eye, in big black letters above the ironmongery. When she sent him this little token she was well over fifty, and the address on the back of the envelope showed that she still lived in the same street, the same house.

She was there to this day. He sometimes imagined her, a little old woman dressed in black, trotting along, close to the house walls, on her way to early mass on some gray morning.

Since that first medal she had formed the habit of sending him birthday wishes every year, and the envelope always contained some pious object, a rosary, a religious picture, an *Agnus Dei*.

He had made inquiries through the Prefecture, learned that she was quite well provided for, and had sent her a signed photograph.

The glass panel in the door between the dining room and the kitchen was covered with a red-checked curtain, in the style of a village inn. He could see Gabrielle's shadow moving to and fro on the other side. Madame Blanche had already left, for it was Emile who helped the Premier to get to bed. The telephone had been installed in the house where she lodged, at the near end of the village, and she took her meals at Bignon's inn, known nowadays as the Hôtel Bignon, where the policemen put up.

He heard Emile's footsteps, then caught sight of his

shadow against the curtain, as he came into the kitchen from out of doors, announcing:

"All right now! It's working."

"What's working?" Gabrielle mumbled.

"The radio."

The old cook wasn't interested in the radio; she went on grilling herrings for the servants' supper, while Emile slumped down on the bench and poured himself a glass of cider.

Since five o'clock the Premier had been deliberately avoiding the thought of Chalamont, who had been mentioned in the Paris-Inter broadcast, and the telephone call had come like a dispensation of Providence to take his mind off the subject. In any case he had trained himself to accomplish that feat easily: to turn his thoughts in a given direction and prevent them from straying in any other.

It was too soon to think about Philippe Chalamont, for there were only rumors so far, and even if the President of the Republic asked him to form a Cabinet, Chalamont would not necessarily agree.

Young Marie stood behind him, vacant-eyed, watching him eat; she could hardly have looked sloppier, and it was obvious she would never learn, but would end up sooner or later in her right place, as a barmaid in some harborside café at Fécamp or Le Havre.

"Will Monsieur take a *tisane*?"

"I *always* take a *tisane*."

He went off, with hunched shoulders, not knowing what to do with his arms, which, now that his body had shrunk, had become too long. He used to say to himself:

"If man is descended from the apes I must be returning to my origin, for I look more and more like a gorilla."

Emile had put the loud-speaker on the table, with the extension cord going out through the window frame and connected up with the car radio. When the time came for the news, he would only have to switch on. Emile had thought of this himself, during their first year at Les Ebergues. With a storm just like tonight's blowing, the electricity had failed in the middle of an unusually violent debate in the U.N.

The Premier, furious, was prowling around his office, lit, as now, by an oil lamp, except that they hadn't yet found a globe for it, when Emile had knocked on the door.

"If you will allow me, sir, I would like to make a suggestion. Have you thought of the radio in the car, sir?"

On that occasion he had gone out in the dark, swathed in a rug made of wildcat skins—it was a present from the Canadians—and sat in the back of the Rolls, with the dial of the radio as his only light, until the midnight news.

Since then Emile, who enjoyed playing the handyman, had improved the system, bought a second loud-speaker which only needed connecting with the radio set.

There was no electric failure in Paris, and they probably didn't realize that in Normandy the storm was bringing down trees, telegraph poles, and chimneys. Journalists and photographers were mounting guard in the courtyard of the Elysée, where it was raining, and in the corridors and bar of the Chamber little knots of overexcited Deputies were forming in the window nooks.

An anxious calm would be reigning in the Ministries, where every crisis improved or endangered the prospects of promotion of hundreds of civil servants, and the Prefects, each in his own fief, would be waiting with equal anxiety for the seven-fifteen news.

For forty years, on such occasions, it had invariably been his name that had been put forward in the last resort. He had usually remained secluded in his flat on the Quai Malaquais, the one he had moved into when first called to the Bar.

Milleran had not been his secretary in those days. She was still a little girl, and in her place, waiting silently in the room with him, ready to jump on the telephone, there had been an ungainly young man with a pointed nose, whose name was Chalamont.

There was a difference of twenty years in their ages, and it had been curious to see how the secretary took on the gait, voice, posture, and even the mannerisms of his chief. Over the telephone it was so marked that most people were taken in and addressed him as "Minister." Wasn't it even stranger, perhaps, to note that the face of this lad of twenty-five was as impassive as that of a middle-aged man who had had many years to harden him?

Was it because of this mimicry, because one could feel that his admiration was intensely sincere, that the Premier had kept him on, carrying him along from one Ministry to the next, first as attaché, then as secretary, finally as Principal Private Secretary?

Chalamont was now Deputy for the sixteenth arrondissement, and lived with his wife, who had brought him a large fortune, in a flat overlooking the Bois de Boulogne. He didn't need to make a living out of politics, but he stuck to the political world from choice, some people said as a vice, for he was a savage fighter.

And yet, though he was the leader of quite a large group, he had only once been in the Cabinet, and then only for three days.

Wasn't it characteristic of him that on that occasion he had chosen to be Minister of the Interior, and have the police records at his disposal?

What the public, and a good many political men, did not know was that during those three days there had been an almost uninterrupted series of telephone calls between Les Ebergues and Paris, and that Bénouville had noticed an unusual number of cars whose number plates indicated that they came from the Seine Department, all making for the house on the cliff.

On the morning when the new government had presented itself in the Chamber there had been no electric failure, and the old man of Les Ebergues had been listening, with a gleam of ever-increasing satisfaction in his eyes, to the course of the debate.

The proceedings had lasted just three hours, and the newborn government had been defeated before Chalamont had even had time to move into his office in the Place Beauvau.

Was the Premier still as powerful as that today? Hadn't people rather forgotten the statesman who had retired haughtily to the Normandy coast and whom children, learning about him at school, imagined to have died long ago?

"May I go to dinner, sir?"

"By all means, Milleran. Tell Emile to turn on the radio at ten past seven."

"Will you need me?"

"Not this evening. Good night."

She had a room between Gabrielle's and Emile's, above the kitchen, and young Marie slept in a small ground-floor room, once a storeroom, which had had a window put in its outside wall.

Alone in the book-lined rooms, only two of which had any light this evening, the Premier moved slowly from one to another, scrutinizing certain shelves, certain bindings, now and then running his finger along the top of a volume. One day young Marie had caught him at this kind of suspicious inspection, and she had asked:

"Have I left some dust?"

He had turned slowly toward her, had given her a long stare before replying briefly:

"No."

It might be she, it might be Milleran, or even Emile, and he wouldn't allow himself to suspect one of them rather than another. He had known about it for months, and felt sure there must be at least two of them hunting, one inside the house and one outside, possibly one of the detectives.

He had been neither surprised nor annoyed, and at first it had rather amused him.

For a man who had nothing left to do except die in a manner worthy of the legend that had grown up around him, this was an unhoped-for diversion.

Who? Not only, *who* was ferreting among his books and papers, looking for something, but *who* had set them to it?

He, too, had been Minister in the Place Beauvau, not for three days but, on several occasions, for months, once for two whole years. So he knew the methods of the Rue des Saussaies as well as he knew the records that were such a temptation to fellows like Chalamont.

Nearly every evening since making his discovery, he had distributed through the four rooms a number of reference marks, "witnesses," as he privately termed them, which were sometimes no more than a thread of cotton, a hair,

a scarcely visible scrap of paper, sometimes a volume just
slightly out of alignment.

In the mornings he made his round, like a fisherman
going to pick up his lobster pots, for he had always forbidden anybody to go into those rooms before he did. The
housework was left until he was up, and then done not with
a vacuum cleaner, which he hated the noise of, but with
broom and feather duster.

Why had they thought first of all of the memoirs of
Saint-Simon? One morning he had found that one of the
volumes, which he had pushed in by a quarter of an inch
the previous evening, was back in line with the rest. The detectives living at the Bénouville inn could not have guessed
that Saint-Simon had been among his favorite bedside
books all his life.

A calf-bound folio of Ovid, whose size would have made
it an ideal hiding place, had been handled next, then, a few
weeks later, an entire row of illustrated books on art, most
of which were bound in boards.

It had all begun about the time when he had told a foreign journalist that he was writing his memoirs.

"But you have already published them, Premier, and they
were even printed in the biggest magazine in my country."

He was in a good humor that day. He liked the journalist. It amused him to give the fellow a scoop, if only to annoy
certain other journalists whom he couldn't stand.

"My official memoirs have been published," he retorted.
"So you didn't tell the whole truth in them?"

"Perhaps not the *whole* truth."

"And you're going to tell it this time? Really the whole
of it?"

His mind was not made up then. It had all been in the

nature of a joke. He had indeed begun, for his own amusement, to write a commentary on the events he had been
mixed up with, giving little sidelights that no one else knew
about.

It had become a kind of secret game, and now he was
still wondering, with amusement, who would find those
notes in the end, and how.

They were already looking. So far, nobody had looked
in the right place.

Naturally the entire press had printed the information
about his "secret notebooks," as they were called, and the reporters had come to Les Ebergues in greater numbers than
ever before, all asking the same questions:

"Are you going to publish during your lifetime?... Will
you have them held back until some years after your death,
as the Goncourts did?... Are you revealing the shady side
of twentieth-century politics, foreign as well as domestic?... Are you bringing in other world statesmen you've
known?..."

He had given evasive replies. The journalists had not
been alone in the interest they took in those memoirs,
and several important personages, including two generals,
whom he hadn't seen for a number of years, had visited the
Normandy coast that summer, as though by chance, and felt
impelled to pay their respects to him.

They were no sooner seated in his study than he began
to wonder when the question would come. They'd all taken
the same tone, casual, joking.

"Is it true you've written something about me in your
private papers?"

All he would say was:

"The press reports were very exaggerated. I've only just

begun to jot down notes, and I don't know yet whether anything will come of it. . . . "

"I know some people who are trembling at the idea."

He would reply innocently:

"Ah!"

He knew what was being said on the quiet, what two
newspapers had had the temerity to say in print: that,
piqued at being left in silence, forgotten, he was revenging
himself by suspending this undefined threat over the heads
of hundreds of the Establishment.

For a few days he had even wondered whether there
might not be a grain of truth in this, and his conscience had
been uneasy.

But if it had been like that he wouldn't have gone on,
and he would in fairness have destroyed the pages he had
already written.

He had reached an age at which a man can no longer
fool himself.

It was actually because of Chalamont, his former secretary, whose name would be mentioned over the radio in a
few minutes, that he had decided against drawing back; not
that Chalamont was important, but his case was typical.

As had been more or less announced just now, would
not the President of the Republic probably be going to give
him the job of forming a government?

Chalamont would undoubtedly remember that once
when his old chief was asked about his prospects of receiving a portfolio, he had replied curtly:

"He'll never be Premier as long as I'm alive."

After pausing as he always did when he wanted to stress
the importance of his pronouncements, he had added:

"Nor when I'm dead, either."

At this very moment, when the storm outside was wrenching at the roof tiles and a shutter was banging, Chalamont would be at the Elysée and the journalists would be in the rain-swept courtyard, waiting for his answer.

The door of the Rolls opened and closed again. Almost at once, the loud-speaker, standing on the oak table, began to crackle faintly, and the Premier sat down in his Louis-Philippe armchair, folded his hands, closed his eyes, and waited too.

CHAPTER 3

FIRST OF ALL CAME THE NEWS AGENCIES' REPORTS, terse and impersonal:

"Paris . . . Latest developments in the political situation . . . At five o'clock this afternoon the President of the Republic received Monsieur Philippe Chalamont, leader of the Left Independent Group, at the Elysée and asked him to form a coalition Cabinet. The Deputy for the sixteenth arrondissement postponed his reply until tomorrow morning. At the end of this news bulletin we shall broadcast a short interview with Monsieur Chalamont by our representative, Bertrand Picon. . . .

"Saint-Etienne . . . The fire that broke out last night in an electrical equipment factory . . . "

The Premier sat motionless, no longer listening, keeping an eye on a log which was threatening to roll onto the floor. Two or three gusts of wind made it shake and crackle, and finally he got up, squatted down by the hearth, cautiously, for he was not forgetting his leg, took the tongs, and tidied up the fire.

He would have half an hour to wait. The French radio correspondents were speaking, one after another, from London, New York, Budapest, Moscow, Beirut, Calcutta. Before settling into his armchair again he took several slow turns around the table and regulated the wick of the oil lamp.

"And now we come to today's sport. . . . "

Another five minutes and it would be Chalamont's turn.

When the moment arrived there was a brief interruption while they switched from the live broadcast to the tape, for the interview was a recorded one. That was perceptible from the sound, which had changed, and from the voices, which had a different timbre, so that one could tell that the two speakers had been out of doors.

"*Ladies and gentlemen, it is a quarter to six and we are in the courtyard of the Elysée, I and a number of newspaper reporters. . . . This wet, windy day is the eighth that has gone by since the government fell, and as usual Paris has been full of gossip.*

"*At the present moment the question is: Are we to have a Chalamont government?*

"*Just over half an hour ago, Monsieur Philippe Chalamont, summoned by Monsieur Cournot, arrived in his car and strode rapidly past us and up the steps, with no more than a wave of his hand to indicate that he had nothing to say to us yet.*

"*The leader of the Left Independent Group and Deputy for the sixteenth arrondissement, whose photograph has often appeared in the papers, is a vigorous man who looks younger than his sixty years. He is very tall, with a bald forehead, and rather stout. . . .*

"*As I said before, it is raining. There is not room for all of us under the porch of the main entrance, where the doorkeepers are indulgently turning a blind eye to our presence, and a charming lady among our number has valiantly opened a red umbrella. . . .*

"*Outside the gate, in the Faubourg Saint-Honoré, the Municipal Guards are keeping a discreet watch over the small crowd that gathers in little knots and disperses again. . . .*

Hello!... I believe ... Yes ... Is that he, Danet?... Thanks, old man....

"*Excuse me ... I'm told that at this very moment Monsieur Chalamont is crossing the immense hall of the Elysée, which is dazzling with light.... Yes, as I bend down I can see him myself.... He's just put on his overcoat.... He's taking his gloves and hat from the attendant. Close to us, his chauffeur has opened the door of the car.... So in an instant we shall know whether he has taken on the the job of forming a Cabinet....*"

There was the sound of a bus going past, then some confused noises and a kind of scuffle, with voices in the background:

"*Don't push ...*"

"*Let me through, old man ...*"

"*Monsieur Chalamont ...*"

Then again the well-pitched, faintly conceited tones of Bertrand Picon.

"*Minister, I would like you, sir, to tell our listeners ...*"

Although Chalamont had only been a Cabinet Minister for three days and, indeed, had spent only a few hours in the office in the Place Beauvau, ushers, journalists, and all habitués of the Palais-Bourbon would address him for the rest of his life as "Minister," just as others, simply because they had once presided over some vague Parliamentary Committee, were known as "President."

"*... first of all, for what reason Monsieur Cournot sent for you this afternoon.... I am correct, am I not, in thinking that it was in order to ask you to form a coalition Cabinet?...*"

The old man's fingers whitened as he sat still in his armchair. He heard an embarrassed cough, and then, at last, the voice:

"*—As a matter of fact the President of the Republic has done me the honor . . .* "

A car hooted, emerging from the confused background noises. What gave the old man at Les Ebergues the impression that Chalamont was peering around, in the wet, gloomy courtyard of the Elysée, as though looking for a ghost? There was a strange note of anxiety in his voice. For the first time, after a lifetime of effort, he had been asked to lead his country's government, and he knew that someone, somewhere, was listening, he couldn't possibly fail to think of it, someone who was silently bidding him to refuse.

Another voice, not Picon's, probably that of a journalist, broke in:

"*May we tell our readers that you have agreed and that you will begin your interviews this evening?*"

Even over the radio, especially over the radio, which is merciless, one could sense a blank, a hesitation; then came laughter, inexplicable at such a moment, and whispers of mirth.

"*Ladies and gentlemen, you can hear the press representatives laughing, but I assure you their amusement has no connection with what has been said on either side. A moment ago Monsieur Chalamont suddenly flapped his hand, as though something had touched it unexpectedly, and we noticed that the umbrella of the lady journalist I told you about was dripping on it. . . . Excuse that aside, Minister, but our listeners wouldn't have understood. . . . Would you please speak into the microphone. . . . You were asked whether . . .* "

"*I thanked the President for the honor he had done me, which I very much appreciate . . . and . . . er . . . I asked him*" (a car hooted very close by, in the Faubourg Saint-Honoré)

"... to allow me ... to allow me to think things over and give
him my reply in the morning...."

"But your group met at three o'clock this afternoon, and it
is rumored that you were given a free hand...."

"That is the case...."

It seemed as though he were trying to get away, to dive
into his car, whose door the chauffeur was still holding open.

The speaker had felt impelled to mention that he was
rather stout because that was what struck one at the first
glance; he had the portly appearance characteristic of men
who were thin for a good deal of their lives and don't know
how to carry off the fat that has accrued to them. His double
chin and low-slung belly looked like padding, whereas his
nose, for instance, was still sharp and his lips were so thin as
to be almost nonexistent.

"Minister, sir ..."

"With your permission, gentlemen ..."

"One last question. Can you tell us who are the chief people you intend to consult?"

Another blank. They might have cut out these pauses
when they edited the tape. Had they refrained because they,
too, realized that there was something unusual and pathetic
about such hesitancy? The photographers on the steps must
be sending up a barrage of flashlights during the interview,
lighting up the driving rain and bringing Chalamont's face
out of the darkness for a second to emphasize its pallor and
anxiety.

"I can't answer that question yet."

"Will you be seeing anyone this evening?"

"Gentlemen ..."

He was almost suppliant, as he struggled to escape from
the cluster of people who were cutting him off from his car.

Suddenly there came a sharp, piercing voice which might have been that of a little boy, but the Premier recognized it as belonging to a highly esteemed reporter, as it snapped:

"Aren't you intending to spend the night on the road?"

An unintelligible stutter.

"Gentlemen, I have nothing more to say. . . . Excuse me. . . . "

Another pause. The slam of a car door, the sound of an engine, the crunch of gravel, and finally, silence; then Bertrand Picon again, speaking in more measured tones from a different setting, the studio:

"You have been listening to the interview with Monsieur Philippe Chalamont which was recorded as he left the Elysée. Refusing to make any further comment, the Deputy for the sixteenth arrondissement drove back to his home on the Boulevard Suchet where a group of journalists, undismayed by the bad weather, is mounting guard outside the door. We shall know tomorrow whether France has any immediate prospect of emerging from the deadlock which has now existed for over a week, and whether we are soon to have a government.

"Paris-Inter calling. . . . That is the end of the news. . . . "

Music. The door of the Rolls opened and there came a tap at the window, outside which Emile's face could be seen as a pale blur. A sign told him that he could turn off the radio, and the noise of the storm grew stronger.

In the soft light of the oil lamp the old man's face looked haggard, and his immobility was so striking that when, shortly afterwards, Emile came into the study, bringing with him a little of the cold and damp from outside, he stopped with a frown.

The Premier kept his eyes closed, and Emile, standing at the entrance of the tunnel, gave a cough.

"What is it?"

"I came to ask you whether I'm to leave the Rolls outside until the final news?"

"You can put it in the garage."

"You're sure you don't want . . . ?"

"Quite sure. Is Milleran at table?"

"She's having dinner."

"And so are Gabrielle and young Marie?"

"Yes, sir."

"Had your supper?"

"Not yet. . . . "

"Then go and get it."

"Thank you, sir."

Just as the man was going away, he called him back:

"Who's on duty tonight?"

"Justin, sir."

Inspector Justin Aillevard was a fat, melancholy little man. It was no use sending him word to go to bed, or even suggesting that he might come in out of the rain, for he took his orders from the Rue des Saussaies and it was to the Rue des Saussaies that he was responsible. The most that Gabrielle could manage now and again was to invite the policeman on duty to come into the kitchen for a moment and give him a glass of cider or calvados, according to the weather, and perhaps a slice of cake still warm from the oven.

As the Premier did not say he could go, Emile still waited, and he had to wait a long time before hearing the hesitant words:

"We may perhaps have a visitor tonight. . . . "

"Do you want me to stay up?"

The chauffeur realized that for some mysterious reason

his reactions were being closely watched, and that those eyes, open now, were studying his face more keenly than usual.

"I don't know yet ... "

"I'm quite ready to stay up.... You know it doesn't bother me.... "

In the end he was dismissed, with a touch of impatience: "Get along and eat."

"Very good, sir."

This time he really did go, and a moment later he was straddling the bench to sit down at the kitchen table.

Could Loubat—the name had just come back to him—the sharp-voiced journalist who'd questioned Chalamont, have information that the Premier didn't possess? Or had he merely spoken on the off-chance, on the strength of thirty years spent behind the scenes in the Chamber of Deputies and the various Ministries?

It was twelve years since the two politicians had last come face to face. During the Premier's last period in Paris they had occasionally been at the same sitting at the Palais-Bourbon, but one was on the government bench and the other with his Parliamentary group, and they had taken care not to meet.

Their quarrel, as some people called it, or, as others put it, the hatred between them, was well known, but a variety of theories existed as to its origin.

An explanation favored by young parliamentarians, those of the new generation, was that the Premier accused his former colleague of having been the mainspring of the plot that had kept him out of the Elysée.

In the first place, that credited Chalamont with an influence he was far from possessing; in the second place it

revealed ignorance of the fact that for certain definite reasons it would have been political suicide for Chalamont to
have taken such an attitude.

The Premier preferred not to dwell on that episode of his
life, even though his motives had been very different from
the ones attributed to him.

He had been at the apex of his glory in those days. His
energy, his uncompromising spirit, and the measures he
had relentlessly adopted had saved the country from the
very brink of the abyss. His photograph, surmounted by
a tricolor cockade or ribbon, was enshrined in the shop
windows of every town in France, and allied nations were
inviting him to triumphant receptions.

When the Head of the State died, he had been on the
point of retiring from political life, in which he had spent
long enough, and it was neither vanity nor ambition that
had made him change his plans.

He had talked about it to Fumet one day later on, when
he was dining with the Professor in his flat in the Avenue
Friedland. He'd been in a good temper that evening, though
still with the slightly crabby undertone that characterized
his personality.

"You see, my dear Doctor, there is a fact which is over-
looked not only by the public, but by those who shape public
opinion, and it always bothers me when I read the life of a
famous statesman. People talk about the leader's interests,
his pride or his ambition. What they forget, or refuse to see,
is that beyond a certain stage, a certain level of success, a
statesman is no longer himself, he becomes the prisoner of
public events. Those aren't quite the right words . . . "

Fumet, who had a nimble mind and who was the doctor,
and in most cases the personal friend, of everybody who

was anybody in the country, was watching him through a cloud of cigar smoke.

"Let's put it this way, that there comes a moment, a rung of the ladder, at which a man's personal interests and ambitions become merged with those of his country."

"Which is tantamount to saying that at a certain level treason, for example, becomes unthinkable?"

He had sat for a moment in silence. He would have liked to give a definite, clear-cut reply, and he followed up his thought as far as he could:

"Sheer treason, yes."

"On condition, I take it, that the man is worthy of his office?"

At that moment he had thought of Chalamont, and answered:

"Yes."

"And that isn't always the case?"

"It always would be, if it were not for certain forms of cowardice which are to some extent collective, and above all, for certain kinds of indulgence."

It was in this spirit that he had felt it his duty to stand for the Presidency of the Republic. Contrary to the rumors that had been spread, he had had no intention of changing the Constitution, or of reducing the prerogatives of the executive.

He was perhaps said to have brought a rather sterner spirit into politics, and those who knew him best had spoken of his secular Jansenism.

He hadn't gone to Versailles himself. He had stayed in his flat on the Quai Malaquais, alone with Milleran, Chalamont's successor.

At the luncheon that followed the opening meeting

his chances were already being discounted, and with a
few words over the telephone he had withdrawn from the
contest.

Three weeks afterwards he left Paris, a voluntary exile,
and though he kept his bachelor flat he hadn't set foot in it
since.

Had his departure made Chalamont think he could get
forgiveness more easily, and that the road was at last open?
The Deputy for the sixteenth arrondissement had put out
feelers, and his way of doing it had been typical of the man.
He hadn't written, or come to Les Ebergues. The frontal attack was never in his line, and his schemes were usually very
long-term affairs.

One morning the Premier had been surprised to see
his son-inlaw, François Maurelle, arrive at Les Ebergues, by
himself. He was a nonentity, colorless but conceited, who
had been working as a surveyor somewhere outside Paris
when Constance first met him.

Why had she chosen him? She wasn't pretty, a bit on the
masculine side, and her father had always regarded her with
a curiosity in which there was more surprise than affection.

Maurelle's own intentions had been clear; less than a
year after the marriage he had informed his father-in-law
that he intended to stand for Parliament.

He had been defeated twice: the first time in the
Bouches-du-Rhône, where he had been ill-advised to stand
at all; next time at Aurillac, where at a second attempt he
had finally worn down the voters' resistance.

The couple lived in the Boulevard Pasteur, in Paris, and
spent their summer holidays in the Cantal.

He was a big, flabby chap, always dressed up to the
nines, always with his hand held out and his lips ready to

smile, the kind of fellow who won't express his views even on the most harmless subject without first peering at you to try to guess what yours may be.

The Premier had done nothing to help him, merely staring at him as malevolently as if he'd been a slug in the salad.

"I was at Le Havre, after driving a friend to the boat, and I thought I'd just like to drop in on you ... "

"No."

That was an unpopular trick of his. His "no" was celebrated, for he brought it out frequently, without anger or any other inflection. It wasn't even a contradiction: it simply took note of an almost mathematical fact.

"I assure you, my dear Premier ... "

The old man waited with a faraway gaze.

"As a matter of fact ... Though in any case I'd have come specially ... It just so happens that the day before yesterday I was talking about my trip to a bunch in the Chamber ... "

"To whom?"

"Give me a little time ... And please don't think I'm trying to influence you.... "

"That would be impossible."

"I know.... "

He smiled, and if one had slapped his face one's fingers would perhaps have got stuck in those plump, flaccid cheeks.

"I suppose I ought not to have done it—I hope you don't mind.... I only promised to give you the message.... It's from somebody who used to work with you and who's very much upset about a situation ... "

The Premier had picked up a book from the table and seemed to be absorbed in it, paying no further attention to his visitor.

"As you'll have guessed, it's Chalamont.... He doesn't bear you any grudge, he realizes that you acted for the best, but to quote his own words he thinks he has perhaps been sufficiently punished.... He's not a young man now.... He could aim very high if you ... "

The book snapped shut.

"Did he tell you about the luncheon at Melun?" asked the Premier as he rose to his feet.

"No. I know nothing about the business. I suppose he did something he shouldn't, but it's twenty years ago now ... "

"Sixteen."

"Excuse me. It was before I was in the Chamber. Do you think I may tell him ... "

"That the answer is no. Good evening."

With that, leaving his son-in-law stranded, he had gone into his bedroom and shut the door.

This time Chalamont wouldn't rest content with sending him a fellow like Maurelle. This was not a question of some secondary post in a Cabinet. The stake now was the ambition he'd been pursuing all his life, the part he'd been rehearsing since he was twenty years old, and which he'd at last been invited to play.

The years he had spent as the Premier's secretary, or rather as his fervent disciple, his marriage to a rich woman, the humdrum work he had done for various committees, the elocution lessons he had taken, at the age of forty, with a teacher from the Conservatoire, and the three languages he had mastered, his tremendous erudition, his foreign travels, his entire life, private and social, all of this had been undertaken solely with a view to the high office to which he would one day accede.

And now, as he stood in the courtyard of the Elysée,

under the rain that was making its cobbles glisten, someone had asked him an innocent yet terrible question:

"*Aren't you intending to spend the night on the road?*"

The man who put that question had known that it would fling Chalamont into confusion.

At this moment the arbiter of his fate was an old man, cut off from the outside world even more completely than usual owing to an electric failure and a telephone break-down, who sat in a Louis-Philippe armchair, with the sea beating against the cliff hard by and squalls of wind threat-ening, at ever-diminishing intervals, to carry away the roof of his house.

Twice, three times, the Premier muttered to himself:

"He won't send anybody."

Then, hesitantly:

"He'll come...."

At once he would have liked to take back his words, for he was not so sure. At forty years old, or at fifty, he had still believed himself to be a good judge of men, and would pro-nounce his verdicts without hesitation or remorse. At the age of sixty he had already been less sure of himself, and now he did no more than grope in the dark for momentary truths.

The definite fact was that Chalamont had not refused the Head of State's invitation. He had got himself a breath-ing space. But that couldn't mean that he intended to defy the taboo laid on him by his former chief.

So he hadn't lost hope....

A cracking sound from outside the house—a branch be-ing maltreated by the wind—roused a doubt, a suspicion, in his mind, and although he had already made his daily inspection he got up and walked through Milleran's office, where the lamp threw a dim light into the two rooms beyond. He went to the fourth room, the farthest from his bedroom; here were the books he never opened, but kept because they were presentation copies with inscriptions, or because they were rare editions.

He was no bibliophile and had never bought a book for the sake of its binding or its rarity. He had never indulged in any passion, craze, or hobby, as the English call it, holding aloof from fishing, shooting, and all other sports, sailing and climbing, novels, paintings, and the theatre, and he had wanted to reserve his whole energy for his duties as a statesman, a little as Chalamont, his pupil, had tried to do.

He had not even wanted to be a father, his married life having lasted hardly three years, and though he had had mistresses he had only looked to them for relaxation, an interval of charm and elegance usually, with just a touch of affection, and had never repaid them with anything more than brief, condescending attention.

In this respect, too, legend was far from the truth, especially on the subject of Marthe de Créveaux, the Countess as she was called at the time, and as her faithful admirers continued to call her after her death.

Would he go on to the end of his notes, his genuine memoirs, which in a way were corrections, or would he leave behind him, uncaring, the image that had grown up by slow degrees and had so completely ousted the real person?

Before bending down to the lowest shelf he crossed the room and drew the curtain, for he never allowed the shutters to be closed until he was getting into bed. Once they were closed he felt as though he were shut up in a box, already removed from the world, and the irregular throbbing of his heart would sometimes seem to his ears like an alien sound. Once, in fact, he had listened more attentively, convinced that it had stopped beating.

The *Roi Pausole* was in its place, a very handsome edition illustrated by distinctly licentious drawings; the artist had sent him this inscribed copy when he was Premier. It was printed on handmade Japanese paper, in unbound sections, each followed by its set of loose-leaf illustrations, and protected by a gray cardboard case.

Would it occur to anyone, when he died, to leaf through his books, one by one, before sending them to the Salle Drouot to be scattered by auction?

His daughter, from what he knew of her, wouldn't open them. Nor would her husband. They might perhaps keep a few as souvenirs, but certainly not this one, for the illustrations would shock them.

It was amusing to imagine the fate of documents of the greatest importance, carried by the chances of an auction into the hands of people who hadn't even known they existed.

Not long ago he had moved Chalamont's confession, written in a feverish hand on paper with the heading of the Prime Minister's office, and had put it into this book by Pierre Louÿs, He had chosen that particular book because he had suddenly noted a resemblance between his one-time secretary, now that he'd put on flesh, and the King of Boeotia as depicted by the illustrator.

Several of his hiding places had been selected owing to equally unexpected comparisons, many of them humorous. As for the celebrated memoirs, they were not in the form of a connected manuscript, as everyone imagined; they were simply notes, explanations, and corrections, in tiny writing, in the margins of the three volumes of his official autobiography. Only instead of the French edition he had used the American one, which stood on the shelf side by side with the Japanese edition and some twenty other translations.

The paper he was looking for was in its place, in the second section, between pages 40 and 41, and the ink had had time to fade a bit.

"*I, the undersigned, Philippe Chalamont . . .* "

Hearing a sound, he started and put the book back in place, as furtively as a child surprised in a prank. It was only Emile, turning down his bed for the night, and Emile could not see him from the bedroom.

Had the man been surprised at not finding him in his study, and had he glanced into Milleran's office? If so, was he wondering what the Premier could possibly be up to in the semidarkness of the fourth room?

Had Chalamont tried to telephone from Paris? Had he set out, with his chauffeur? In that case, even with the bad weather, it would hardly take him more than three hours.

"Young Marie wants to know if she can go to the village."

He replied indifferently:

"Let her go."

"She says her mother's going to have a baby during the night."

Young Marie already had six or seven brothers and sisters, he wasn't quite sure how many, and it didn't matter anyhow. But an idea did occur to him.

"How will they let the doctor know?"

The nearest doctor was at Etretat, and it would not be possible to telephone to him.

"It's not the doctor who's delivering her, it's old Babette. . . . "

He didn't ask who Babette was. He'd only meant to offer the car. But if they didn't need it . . .

"Will you be going to bed as usual?"

"Yes, at ten o'clock." He had no reason for making any change in the pattern of his life. He invariably went to bed at ten o'clock, whether tired or not, and invariably got up, winter and summer alike, at half past five in the morning.

The only member of the household who'd protested against this timetable had been young Marie, although before coming to work for him she'd been a farm-hand and used to get up at four to milk the cows.

"Shall I make up the fire?"

The Premier was edgy, impatient, and this made him angry with himself, for he considered it humiliating to be affected, however slightly, by other people's actions or opinions.

If at the age of eighty-two he still was not secure from outside influences, what hope was there that he ever would be?

This reminded him, for a second, of the death of one of his friends, also an ex-Premier, the most ferocious anticlerical of the Third Republic, who to everyone's astonishment had sent for a priest at the last moment. . . .

He sat down in his usual place and opened Sully's memoirs, while Emile went back to the kitchen, whence he would return in due course to put him to bed.

He didn't read, however. He felt obliged to run over the Chalamont business again, as though searching his own conscience. He always thought of that chapter as entitled "the luncheon at Melun," and there were at least three people, apart from himself, for whom those words had the same sinister ring.

It had happened in June. The weather was bright and hot. Cars were rushing out of Paris, three abreast, toward the Forest of Fontainebleau. The Parisians were off for a day in the country, all unaware of the drama in progress, or else telling themselves, out of habit or from laziness, that those whom they had elected for the purpose would bring it safely to an end.

The financial crisis was probably the blackest the country had been through since the *assignats* of the Revolution. Every expedient had been attempted and they had gone almost hat in hand to beg the help of foreign governments. Every day the country was being drained of its substance, like a body bleeding to death, as the newspapers put it, and the outlook could hardly have been gloomier.

Three weeks earlier the Chamber had granted full powers to the government, after a stormy and inglorious night sitting. Every morning since then the papers had been asking:

"How are they going to use them?"

The Governor of the Bank of France was sending hourly messages, each more alarming than the last. Ascain, the Finance Minister, who had known, when he accepted that office, that it would bring him nothing but unpopularity and might mean the end of his political career, was conferring every morning with the Premier.

After the disastrous experiments made by previous governments, which had lived from day to day, robbing Peter to pay Paul, the only solution was a large-scale devaluation. And even that, if it were to be effective, must happen at the right moment, abruptly and unexpectedly enough to prevent speculation.

There were journalists on guard day and night outside

the Hôtel Matignon in the Rue de Varennes, others in front of the Ministry of Finance in the Rue de Rivoli, and others, again, in the Rue de Valois, where the Governor of the Bank of France lived.

The three men with whom the decision rested were spied upon continually, their words, their mood, their slightest frown interpreted in one way or another.

But little by little the details of the operation had been settled, and all that remained was to fix the new exchange rate and the date of the devaluation.

Nerves were so strained in the Bourse and the foreign Stock Exchanges that the three men responsible ended by being afraid to be seen together for fear it might be taken for a signal.

So they decided to meet for luncheon, one Sunday, at a country house belonging to Ascain, just outside Melun. The appointment had been kept so secret that even their wives did not know about it, and Madame Ascain had not been there to receive her guests.

When he had arrived with Chalamont, who was then his Principal Private Secretary, the Premier had caught a frown on the face of Lauzet-Duché, the Governor of the Bank, but he had not felt called upon to give any reason for bringing the younger man.

Had not Chalamont become almost his shadow? Besides, even before his time, hadn't the Premier felt the need of a silent presence by his side?

The house was built of golden yellow stone; it looked onto a sloping street and was surrounded on three sides by a lovely garden, enclosed by iron railings and walls. It had belonged to Ascain's father, who was a solicitor, and the mark left by the brass plate could still be seen, to the left of the gate.

They had talked of nothing in particular during luncheon, in front of the servants; then they had taken coffee
under a lime tree at the far end of the garden. As they
were more secure from inquisitive ears in that spot than
anywhere else, they had sat on in their wicker armchairs,
around a small table loaded with liqueurs that nobody
touched, to decide the rate of devaluation and fix the zero
hour, which, for technical reasons, had to be Monday, just
before the Bourse closed.

Reaching their decision after weeks of nervous strain,
they had felt so relieved at the idea that matters were now
out of their hands, that Ascain, who was short and plump,
had suddenly pointed to a corner of the garden which was
screened by a row of plane trees and suggested:

"We ought to have a game of skittles."

It was so unexpected, immediately after their serious
conversation, that they had all burst out laughing, including
Ascain, who had thrown out his proposal as a joke.

"There's a proper skittle alley over there, behind the
plane trees," he explained. "My father had a passion for the
game and I still keep the place in order. Like to have a look?"

Lauzet-Duché, a former Inspector of Finance, seldom
relaxed his grave manner, which was enhanced by a square-
cut pepper-and-salt beard.

Still not knowing what they were going to do, the four
men walked across the lawn to the plane trees and there,
indeed, was the skittle alley, with its cindered track and a
big flat stone on which the Finance Minister, bending down,
began to arrange the skittles that were lying about.

"Shall we have a go?"

The newspapers had never got hold of that story. For
more than an hour the four men who had just determined

the fate of the franc and the fortunes of millions of people, had played skittles, at first condescendingly and then with growing enthusiasm.

The next day, fifteen minutes after the opening of the Bourse, the telephone in the Prime Minister's office rang, and Chalamont picked it up, listened in silence, and then said:

"Just a moment, please."

And, turning to his chief:

"Lauzet-Duché wants to speak to you personally.

"Hello?"

"Is that you, Premier?"

Right away he had sensed trouble.

"Forgive me for asking, but I suppose you have told nobody about the decision we took yesterday? And you haven't mentioned it in talking by telephone to Ascain, by any chance?"

"No. Why?"

"I don't know anything definite yet. It's only an impression so far. I'm told that when the Bourse opened there were some rather disturbing dealings...."

"By which bank?"

"It's too soon to say. I'm to have a report every fifteen minutes.... May I ring you back?"

"I shan't budge from my office...."

By half past two over thirty thousand million francs' worth of government stock had been thrown onto the market. By three o'clock the Bank of France was beginning to buy back on the quiet, to prevent a collapse.

Lauzet-Duché, the Rue de Rivoli, and the Premier were in constant touch by telephone, and things reached a point where they wondered if the devaluation would not have to be postponed. This unexpected, unforeseeable speculation had already robbed it of much of its effect.

On the other hand, to draw back now might start a panic.

The Premier was livid when he finally gave the signal, in much the same spirit as a general launching a battle half lost in advance.

This would no longer be a bloodletting operation, affecting the whole of France to a more or less equal extent. Those in the know had already escaped, and what was more they had made huge profits at the expense of the medium and small investors.

During all these discussions Chalamont, as white-faced as his chief, had remained in the office, lighting one cigarette after another and throwing each one away after a few tense puffs.

He was not fat in those days. The caricaturists usually depicted him as a raven.

In a few minutes the news-vendors would be out on the boulevards with special editions. The telephone switchboards at the Premier's house, the Ministry of Finance, and the Bank of France were overwhelmed with calls.

In the spacious office with its carved paneling the Premier sat tapping his blotter with the end of his pencil, his eyes fixed on some detail of a tapestry that hung on the opposite wall.

When at last he stood up, he moved like an automaton.

"Sit down, Chalamont."

His voice was clear, firm, with no more warmth than a machine.

"No. Not there. At my desk, please."

He began to walk up and down, hands behind his back. "Take a pen and a sheet of paper. . . . "

And then he dictated, still walking up and down, with head lowered and hands clasped behind his back, pausing now and then for the right word:

"*I, the undersigned, Philippe Chalamont . . .* "

There was the sound of the pen moving over the paper, the sound of heavy breathing, and, about halfway through the dictation, a sound that resembled a sob.

"I can't . . . "

But the voice cut him short:

"Go on!"

The dictation went on till the bitter end.

CHAPTER 4

"DO YOU REALLY THINK ANYBODY WILL COME in this weather?" muttered Emile skeptically.

It was five minutes to ten. At about half past nine the electric bulbs had lit up feebly, as though trying to come back to life, but after blinking two or three times they had gone out again. A little later, Emile had come in and asked:

"How are you going to manage for the night, sir?"

Seeing that the old man had not immediately realized what he meant, he explained:

"About the light.... I went to the ironmonger's and bought the smallest oil lamp I could find, but I'm afraid even that will be too strong...."

For several months the old man had given up sleeping in the dark; he had a tiny electric light, a special type that had been ordered from Paris. This decision had been taken on his doctor's insistence, after a distressing incident that had deeply humiliated him.

For a long time the doctors, Gaffé and Lalinde, had been urging him not merely to let the nurse stay at Les Ebergues instead of going off to sleep in the village, but to have her all night within call, on a camp bed in his study, for instance, or in the tunnel.

He had flatly, obstinately refused, and Fumet, to whom

they had finally appealed to persuade him, had advised that, on the contrary, he should not be harassed about it.

He understood that for a man who in the whole of his life had never relied on anybody, prizing his independence above everything, the nurse's presence would be tantamount to surrender.

The fact that his chauffeur now turned into a valet, morning and evening, to help him to dress or to get to bed, was quite distressing enough for a man who had always jealously guarded his privacy.

"If I need help I can always ring for it," he had said, indicating the pear-shaped bellpull that hung above the bed.

"Or if not," he had added, "I shall be too far gone for anyone's help."

As a precaution, a very loud bell, shrill as would have befitted a school or a factory, had been placed, not in Emile's room because he might happen to be away, but on the first-floor landing, above the kitchen, so that there were three people to hear it.

But one night that had proved inadequate. In the middle of a nightmare he couldn't entirely shake off, though he was unable to recall it later, he had sat up in bed, in pitch darkness, oppressed, his body bathed in cold sweat, with a sensation of horror that he had never experienced before. He knew there was something he ought to do, that it was agreed on, that they had insisted he must do it, but he couldn't quite remember what it was, he was groping in the dark.

It was like a night he had been through at about eight years old, when he had mumps and had seen the ceiling coming slowly down on top of him, while his eiderdown floated up to meet it.

He struggled with his torpor, wanting to do as they had advised, for he was not hostile to them, whatever they might think, and feeling around in the emptiness, his hand touched a smooth, cold surface. Without realizing it, he had been trying to find the switch of the lamp on his bedside table, and all at once there was a crash on the floor; the tray, the bottle of mineral water, and the glass had been knocked over.

He still couldn't find the cord of the lamp, or the switch. They must have pulled the bedside table farther away; that was a little mystery he would try to clear up later. Meanwhile he felt an urgent, imperative need of action.

Then, leaning forward, he had tipped over and fallen heavily to the floor, all of a piece, landing in a position as ridiculous as on the cliff path the day his left leg had played him that dirty trick.

He could feel splinters of glass all around him, and felt sure that blood was running over his hand, though he didn't know where it came from. He tried to get up, but in vain, there was no strength in his legs, and in the last resort the instinct of the baby in its cot returned to him and he began to shout.

There had been no storm that night. And yet, incredible as it might seem, of the three whose bedrooms were above the kitchen, not so far off, not one had heard him; it was young Marie, so difficult to wake in the morning, who had arrived in her nightdress, smelling of bed. She had turned on the light and stood there for quite a while, as though on her guard, hesitant, suspicious.

Had she believed him to be dead or dying? In the end she, too, had uttered a cry and, instead of giving him a hand, had rushed off upstairs to call the others. When they had come hurrying she had lagged behind, still half frightened.

His wrist had been bleeding, but it wasn't a deep cut. Gaffé had been unable to decide exactly what had been wrong with the Premier.

"It happens to everybody, at any age. Probably a nightmare, brought on by cramp or by a momentary disturbance of the circulation. That would explain why you couldn't get up. . . . "

He had talked again about having Madame Blanche there on a camp bed. The Premier's only concession had been to sleep from then on with a faint light in his room. They'd found him this lamp, hardly bigger than the bulb in a pocket flashlight, and he had grown accustomed to the night light, which had gradually come to form part of his world.

Emile had remembered it this evening, and, without saying anything, had gone down to the village and bought the little oil lamp. As luck would have it, at the very moment when he mentioned it, the electric current made a spasmodic return, died away again, then revived, and at last one could feel, from the brightness of the light, that this time it had come back for good.

"I'll fix you up the oil lamp all the same, just in case . . . "

Morning and evening, for his valeting duties, Emile wore a white linen jacket, and it was probably the way in which the white of the jacket emphasized his black hair and rugged, irregular features that had prompted someone to remark:

"Your man looks more like a thug than a servant. . . . "

He'd been born at Ingrannes, in the depths of the Forest of Orléans, in a family whose men had been gamekeepers, from father to son, for longer than anyone could remember, and he and his brothers had been brought up with the dogs.

But he made one think of a poacher rather than a game-keeper. In spite of his sturdy frame and bulging muscles, he moved about the house more softly than the ethereal Milleran, and a disturbing glint sometimes came into his mocking yet guileless eyes.

The Premier had taken him over the year he had become Foreign Minister. He had found Emile, just released from military service, among the chauffeurs at the Quai d'Orsay, where he had been accepted through the influence of his local "Squire," and he contrasted so strongly with the well-schooled chauffeurs of the Quai that he had found him amusing to watch.

It hadn't been easy to tame him, for at the least approach Emile's face would close up and one would be confronted with an expressionless, irritating wooden mask.

That particular Cabinet had survived for three years, and when it had been finally defeated Emile had muttered hesitantly, hanging his head and fidgeting awkwardly with his cap:

"I suppose there's no chance I could go along with you?"

He had gone along with him for twenty-two years, hanging around him like a dog at his master's heels, and had never spoken of getting married. Presumably he felt no need to do so, but the moment a passable unmarried woman, thin or fat, young or middle-aged, came into his field of vision he would cover her as a cock or a rabbit might, without hesitation but nonchalantly, as though it were part of his natural functions.

The Premier had more than once amused himself by watching his goings on, for he felt that in his dealings with women his chauffeur revealed the same instinct as a poacher dealing with game. When a new victim came along, Emile scarcely appeared to notice her, except that his small black eyes became more set and his movements slower and more silent than usual. He melted into his surroundings at such times, just as a poacher in a forest becomes a tree or a rock, and waited patiently for an hour, a day, or a week, till the propitious moment arrived. Whereupon, with an unerring instinct, he pounced.

Young Marie had certainly had her turn in the first week, if not on the first night, and the Premier would not have been surprised to learn that from time to time Milleran submitted, passively but not unwillingly, to the attentions of the only active male in the household.

Once in Paris he had been almost an eye-witness of one of these forthright conquests, which were an aspect of natural history and had a touch of its rough poetry. It was at the Ministry of Justice, when he was Keeper of the Seals. There had just been some changes in the staff, and on the morning of a big luncheon party a housemaid had arrived from the country, young and dewy, with the bloom still on her.

The great house had been the scene of feverish activity and things had been a bit confused. About nine o'clock in the morning, the Keeper of the Seals had happened to be in a room that was being turned out, just in time to witness the meeting between Emile and the new maid.

He had sensed what was happening. Some people maintain that cock and hen birds communicate with each other by a kind of telepathy, and if so, Emile must have possessed the same faculty of emitting and receiving waves, for on merely catching sight of the girl from behind he made a dead set and his brown pupils contracted.

Later on, as the Premier came out of his own suite, where he had gone to put on his morning coat, he had seen

Emile come into the corridor, emerging from the linen room and closing the door noiselessly behind him; his face was flushed and wore a satisfied expression, and he paused to tidy himself up.

The two men's eyes met, and Emile simply gave an imperceptible wink, as much as to say:

"That's that!"

As though he had just snared a rabbit at the expected spot.

Girls would pester him, claiming that they were pregnant by him. Their fathers would join in now and then, and some of them wrote to the Premier, who still remembered one typical phrase:

"... *and I rely on you, Minister, to see that the skunk puts matters to rights by marrying my daughter....*"

To which Emile would reply, unabashed:

"If a fellow had to marry every girl he put in the family way! ..."

What kind of stories would Emile relate, in future years, to sightseers who came to Les Ebergues? And what did he really think about the old man he served?

"If you've no objection I'll stay in the kitchen and make myself some coffee. Like that, if the gentlemen were to come ..."

Was it he who had hunted through the volumes of Saint-Simon and various other books?

Milleran was equally devoted, and would be much more afflicted by his death. She would find it difficult, at forty-seven, to submit to a new kind of discipline and get used to another employer. Would she yield to the insistence of the publishers who would try to persuade her to write about his private life, so far as she knew it?

Those idiots were unaware that he'd never had any private life, and that at the age of eighty-two his entire store of human relationships—he would not venture upon the word "friendship" or "affection"—consisted of the few people who lived at Les Ebergues.

Gabrielle, whose surname was Mitaine, and who came from the Nièvre, had been married. Widowed at forty, left with one little boy, she had come into his service, and even now she went once a month to Villeneuve-Saint-Georges, to see her son, who was now a man of forty-nine, married, with three children, and worked as head steward in a dining car on the Paris-Ventimiglia line.

Gabrielle was just turned seventy-two. Didn't the thought of death probably haunt her far more than it did her master?

As for young Marie, she would hardly remember the years she had spent working for the "old boy."

Perhaps it would be Madame Blanche who'd remember him longest, although he was more often gruff with her than with any of the others.

In point of fact there were just two people with whom he was on close terms, to whom he really mattered, two who were poles apart and offset each other, so to speak: Xavier Malate, who pursued him with a hatred as tenacious as unrequited love, and was clinging to life so as not to leave it before he did; Eveline, the sandy-haired girl in the Rue Saint-Louis, who, after losing sight of him for sixty years and more, was now sending him consecrated medals every year.

His daughter, his son-in-law, and his grandson didn't count, they had never been part of his existence. They were outsiders, almost strangers.

As for Chalamont . . .

Was he really driving toward Le Havre at this moment? Was the Premier right to be going to bed, when he might perhaps have to get up again at any moment?

"If they come, what room shall I show them into?"

He hesitated for a second. He didn't want to leave Chalamont alone in the studies. This house was not a Ministry, there were no ushers and no waiting room. When a visitor arrived, Milleran left him to wait in one of the book-lined rooms.

At least one visitor came almost every day. Usually only one was allowed, on Professor Fumet's advice, for despite his apparent coldness he exerted himself too much for his guests.

Milleran would say warningly to the newcomer, the moment she let him in:

"Don't keep the Premier for more than half an hour. The doctors say he mustn't tire himself."

Those who arrived like this, or at least those who gained admission, were statesmen from almost every country in the world, historians, university professors, students.

They all had questions to ask. Some of them, those who were writing a book about him, or a thesis, brought along imposing lists of specific questions.

Almost invariably he began the conversation grudgingly, finding it irksome, and seemed to withdraw into his shell.

Then, after a few minutes, he grew lively, and not every visitor noticed that he was now asking the questions instead of submitting to them.

Some people, when the half-hour was up, would conscientiously prepare to take their leave. Or Milleran would appear, silently, in the doorless opening between the two studies.

"We shan't be a minute...."

The minute would stretch out, the half-hour would become an hour, two hours, and sometimes one of these passing visitors, much to his surprise, would be asked to stay to lunch.

This exhausted the Premier, but it cheered him up, and when he was alone again with Milleran he would rub his hands gleefully.

"He came here to pick my brains, and I've been picking his!"

At other times he would inquire jokingly, before an appointment:

"Whom am I to put on my act for today?"

There was some truth in the jest.

"I have to take care of my statue!" he had declared once, in a gay mood.

Without admitting it even to himself, he did take an interest in the impression he was to leave behind him, and there were occasions when the surly retorts for which he was celebrated were not entirely sincere, but formed part of his act. At such times he wouldn't have Milleran around, for he felt rather ashamed of himself in front of her, just as in front of Madame Blanche he felt ashamed of his weakened body.

"Do you need anything else, sir?"

The old man glanced around him. The bottle of water and the glass were in the usual place; so was the sleeping tablet he took every night. The tiny, flat light was switched on. The oil lamp was ready to replace it if need be.

"Good night, sir. I hope I shan't have to disturb you before morning...."

The central light went out, Emile's footsteps drew further

away, the kitchen door opened and closed again, and the room was left to silence and solitude, rendered almost intangible by contrast with the storm outside.

Since he had grown old, he scarcely felt the need of sleep, and for years he had lain in bed like this, for two or three hours every evening, quite still, his eyes shut, in a state of suspended animation.

It was not exactly insomnia. He felt neither annoyance nor impatience and it was by no means disagreeable. Far from it! During the day he sometimes thought with pleasure of the moment when he would thus be left to his own company.

Now he had taken to the little glowing disk it was still more pleasant, for its pinkish light helped, even through his closed eyelids, to create an atmosphere of secret, inner life.

At such times everything softened and mingled, the walls, the furniture, every gleam on which was known to him, the familiar objects he saw without looking at them, whose weight and substance even seemed palpable, the wind, the rain, the cry of a night bird or the sound of the waves at the foot of. the cliff, the creak of a shutter, the movements of somebody undressing in one of the bedrooms, everything, even to the stars twinkling in the silent sky, played its part in a symphony of which he, as he lay apparently inert, was the center and to which his heart beat time.

Was this how death would come, taking him unawares on some not far-distant night? He knew that everybody in the household was expecting to find him, one morning, cold and stiff in his bed. He knew, too, that old people often did die in their sleep, unawares.

He sensed that Milleran's fear was rather that it would

happen at nightfall, while he sat, dozing as it seemed, in his armchair, hands folded on his stomach.

In bed, too, he took that position, the attitude of a dead man prepared for his last journey, and he didn't do it on purpose, but because his body had gradually come to find it comfortable and natural.

Was that a portent?

He didn't believe in portents. He refused to believe in anything, even in the value of his lifework. At least ten times in the course of his life he had felt bound to make a superhuman effort, believing it to be indispensable, and for weeks, months, years he had led a hectic existence, pursuing his objective in the teeth of universal opposition.

On those occasions his energy, his vigorous metabolism, which used to amaze Professor Fumet, would spread not only to his immediate collaborators and to the Chamber, but to the whole country, to the invisible nation, which, after a period of mistrust and uncertainty, would be surprised to find itself following him blindly.

Because of this almost biological faculty, it was always at difficult, desperate moments that he was called in.

How often he had heard the same words uttered by a Head of State driven to the last ditch: "Save France . . . " or: "Save the Republic . . . " or perhaps: "Save freedom . . . "

Every crisis had found him with faith unimpaired, for without that he could have done nothing, a faith so firm that he could sacrifice everything for it, not only himself but others, which had often been harder.

Cold sweat broke out on him even now, he still felt physically unwell, when he recalled his first action as Minister of the Interior; he saw himself, in a black, relentless setting of coal mines and blast furnaces, holding a final parley, all alone between men on strike, whose leaders had turned them into rioters with hate-filled hearts, and the soldiers he had called in.

All the time he was trying to make himself heard, his voice had been drowned by jeering. Then, when he had stopped, a somber and probably grotesque figure, his arms falling helplessly to his sides, there had been a long, vibrant silence, betraying irresolution, hesitation.

The two camps were watching each other closely, defying each other, and suddenly, as though at a signal—it was proved afterwards that there actually was a signal—bricks, cobblestones, and scraps of cast iron came flying through the air, while the soldiers' horses began to whinny and paw the ground.

He knew he would be blamed for his decision to the end of his life, that tomorrow, and for many a long day, most of his countrymen would curse him.

He knew, too, that it was necessary.

"Colonel, give the order to charge."

A week later there were posters on the walls showing him with a hideous grin and with blood dripping from his hands, and the government was overthrown.

But order had been preserved.

Ten times, twenty times, he had withdrawn from the limelight in this way, having completed his task, and had sat, grumpy and silent, on the opposition benches, until he was needed again.

On one occasion some man or other, a nonentity, a kind of Xavier Malate, had come to ask him for a job to which he had no right and, on being refused, had put a bullet through his head in the waiting room, as he left his office.

For some time now, on the advice of his doctors—his

Three Musketeers—he had been taking a light sedative at bedtime, which didn't send him off to sleep at once, but brought on a gradual, delicious drowsiness to which he had grown accustomed.

Sometimes he didn't swallow it immediately, but gave himself the pleasure of prolonging, for half an hour or more, his clearheaded wakefulness, his conversation with himself. He had begun to hoard his life. He felt he had a whole lot of problems left to solve, not only with calm and composure, but in the completely dispassionate mood that he could achieve only at night, in bed.

This was the most secret of all his tasks, concerning no one except himself; he would have liked to finish it before taking his departure, leaving nothing obscure, looking everything straight in the face. Was it not to help himself in this that he had begun to read so many volumes of memoirs, confessions, private diaries?

Coming to the end of one of these books, he was invariably disappointed, irritated, feeling the author had cheated. He wanted pure truth, truth in the raw, as he was trying to find it in his own case, even if it turned out to be sickening or repugnant.

But all the writers he had come across had *arranged* their material, he was far enough on in life to know that. All of them held, believed they held or pretended to hold, a truth, and he, despite his grim search for truth, had not found it.

Just now, hearing Chalamont's voice over the radio, he had been compelled to brace himself. Had he felt any doubt about being in the right when, in his office in the Hôtel Matignon, he had dictated that letter of infamy which his assistant, bathed in sweat so that the whole room stank of it, had taken down, to the last word, and signed?

If he had needed further proof than that submissiveness, he received more than enough in the next few days, when discreet investigation by the Ministry of Finance revealed the fact that Vollard's Bank had been behind the last-minute speculation which had cost the country thousands of million of francs.

Vollard's Bank, in the Rue Vivienne, little known to the general public, was a private firm, working in close co-operation with one of the biggest financial concerns in Wall Street, and Etienne Vollard, its Chairman, was Chalamont's father-in-law.

Didn't the Premier, aware of this family connection, bear a heavy responsibility for taking his assistant to the luncheon party at Melun and insisting that he should be present?

Not for an instant had it occurred to him that Chalamont might betray him. In Ascain's garden, whether before the skittle game or afterwards, he had felt as sure of his assistant as of himself.

Looking at it more closely, his confidence had been in the mission rather than the individual. It all tied up with what he had said to Furnet, in the Avenue Friedland. He had felt certain that Chalamont had once and for all crossed the invisible frontier beyond which the individual man ceases to count, all that matters being the task he has set himself.

That day, the day of the dictation, the Premier's world had tottered and almost collapsed.

He remembered how, the letter written, his Secretary had made for the door and clutched the handle. The idea that he might commit suicide, as the unsuccessful petitioner had done, had not occurred to him and would anyhow not have influenced him.

"Stay here!"

Chalamont still had his back turned, would not wheel around and face him, but he did stop where he was.

"It is impossible for me at present, and will be for some time, to accept your resignation or to kick you out."

He spoke rapidly, in an undertone, jerking out the syllables.

"Imperative reasons make it impossible, unfortunately, for me to bring you into the courts, with your father-in-law and his accomplices."

It was true that legal proceedings, with the resultant scandal, at such a moment, would have destroyed public confidence and led to even greater tragedy.

That, much more than the personal disappointment he had suffered, was the reason for his resentment against Chalamont. The latter knew that whatever might happen, they would have to shelter him, keep quiet, cover up the matter. Vollard's Bank had been gambling on a certainty, and Etienne Vollard, with his pearl-gray top hat, would be seen tomorrow in the owners' stand at Longchamp or Auteuil, where he had horses running. If he won the President of the Republic's Stakes the week after next, the Head of the State could hardly avoid shaking hands with him and congratulating him!

"Until further notice you will carry out your duties as usual, and in public there will be no change in our relationship."

This strain had gone on for a fortnight, though the Premier had been so busy that he could give little thought to his assistant.

When they were alone he avoided speaking to him and, if forced to do so, gave him his instructions in an impersonal tone.

On several occasions Chalamont had opened his mouth as though tormented by the need to say something, and at such times he would gaze pathetically at his chief.

He was no longer a boy, a young man, or even what is known as a budding politician. He was a mature man, his face already lined, and this made his humility disgusting rather than tragic.

How was he behaving in the evening, at dinner with his wife? What had he said to his father-in-law and his partners? What thoughts were revolving in his head when he got into his car and told the chauffeur, seated in front of him, to drive to the Hôtel Matignon?

One morning the Premier found on his desk a letter addressed in his Principal Secretary's writing, and as Chalamont was not there, he left it untouched until the man came in; then he picked up the unopened envelope, holding it between finger and thumb, and tore it into small pieces which he dropped into the wastepaper basket.

Now they were to have their last conversation. It was brief. Without deigning to glance at the other man, as he stood at the far side of the desk, he said:

"From now on you are relieved of your duties with me." Chalamont did not move, and his chief, picking up a file, added:

"I was forgetting.... You can consider our acquaintance at an end.... You may go now."

He had opened the file and picked up the red pencil he used for making notes on documents.

"I said, you may go now!"

"You absolutely refuse to listen to me?"

"*Absolutely*. Leave the room, please."

Lying in bed, he started, for he heard a noise outside.

Straining his ears, he recognized the footsteps of one of the policemen, who was stamping his feet to warm them.

During the last week poor Cournot had appealed to all the political leaders in succession. Some had refused outright. Others had opened negotiations which had dragged on for a day or two. On those occasions arrangements had taken shape, names had been mentioned, lists of probable Ministers had even been put forward, but then each time the structure collapsed at the last moment and the party leaders again began to file through the Elysée.

But where others had failed, Chalamont had a chance of success. His group was a small one, but influential because of its position, halfway between the center and the left, and it had the further advantage of not being committed to any hard-and-fast policy. Moreover, at a time when the different parties held divergent views about economic questions and about wages, the public found something reassuring about the Left Independents.

Among Chalamont's other trump cards were his adaptability, his skill in trimming his sails, and the fact that at the age of sixty he was beginning to count as one of the old guard at the Palais-Bourbon, where he could rely on long-standing friendships and on a network of connections built up by services rendered and minor compromises.

What would the Premier say now, then and there, if they came and asked him:

"Do you think Chalamont can find a way out of the crisis?"

Would he venture to keep silent, or would he frankly say what he thought:

"Yes."

"Do you think that his coming to power would prevent the general strike that is threatening the country?"

There again, the answer was undoubtedly:

"Yes."

When Chalamont had been his right hand he had twenty times helped him to settle disputes with the unions, and although he was the son-in-law of a banker, lived on the edge of the Bois, and sat in the Chamber for the wealthiest arrondissement in Paris, he could handle the workers' representatives as no one else could do.

The Premier tried to halt his argument, which was making him feel uncomfortable, but he wanted to play fair.

"Is Chalamont cut out to be a statesman?"

He hesitated and refused to answer that question, but then it led to another:

"Which of to-day's politicians would make a better Premier?"

Oh, very well! He could think of nobody! Perhaps he was the victim of old age, which ends by distorting even the soundest judgment? If so the newspapers seemed to have grown old with him, which was true to some extent, for many of them still had as their editors, or on their board of directors, men whom the Premier had known in those positions thirty or forty years ago.

However that might be, every time a government fell they, too, would allude to "the great team," lamenting the dearth of men of the former mold, not merely in France but among the leaders of her allies.

Had the world really experienced an age of genuinely great men, of whom the Premier was the sole survivor except for Count Cornelio, the Italian, who was ending his days in a mental home outside Rome?

Again he listened, and this time it was Emile, in the kitchen, who had joggled the bench as he got up. He nearly rang for him, to tell him to go to bed. His thoughts had taken a disagreeable turn, and he was tempted to swallow the pill that lay beside the glass of water.

Outside, the Antifer light, off Etretat, and the lighthouse of Notre-Dame-du-Salut, above Fécamp, must be sweeping the lowering sky with their beams, which would meet almost directly over Les Ebergues.

There would be boats out at sea, with men, stiff in their oilskins, wearing sou'westers and rubber boots, standing on slippery decks and hauling at wet, cold tackle. In the village there would be at least one lighted window, that of the room where young Marie's mother was having her baby.

He hadn't had the curiosity, before getting into bed, to find out whether the telephone was working again. Most likely not. Telephone breakdowns always lasted longer than electricity failures.

It was eleven o'clock. Suppose Chalamont's car had broken down, too, somewhere by the side of the deserted road?

Had he really, during the last few years, been attempting to get back the confession he had signed in such dramatic circumstances?

Save for that paper, already yellowing, there was no evidence against him except the bare word of an old man whom many people now thought of as disappointed, embittered, with a lasting grudge against the world for not allowing him to end his career as President of the Republic.

Ascain had died in his fine house at Melun, to which he had retired after being heavily defeated at the polls, and where he had presumably spent his last years in playing skittles. He had left no memoirs. He had left no money either, and his two sons, one a vet and the other a traveler in patent medicines, had sold the property that had come down to them from their grandfather, the solicitor.

Ascain would bring no charge now. As for Lauzet-Duché, he had been the first to go, carried away by a stroke while making a speech at the end of a banquet in Brussels.

The others didn't know. In any case, how many still survived, even of the civil servants who had been merely on the outskirts of the affair, each knowing only one small part of it?

All that remained was a scrap of paper.

Was that what someone had been seeking at Les Ebergues for several months past? Up and down the house, in other books besides *Le Roi Pausole*, there were a hundred documents as dangerous to various people as that one was to Chalamont. Anyone who spends a great part of his life, particularly a life as long as his own, not only in the political arena but in the wings as well, is bound to witness any number of cowardly and disreputable actions.

And if someone were to ask him now:

"Do you know one single politician who in the entire course of his career has never ... "

He cut his thought off short, as he used to cut off other people's words.

"No!"

He wasn't going to play that game. He'd been about to fall into his own trap, and with a brusque movement he propped himself on one elbow, seized the pill, and swallowed it with a mouthful of water.

He needed sleep and wanted to get to sleep quickly, without thinking any longer.

The last picture to drift more or less coherently through his mind was that of a man, whose features he could not distinguish, lying in a hospital bed. This was supposed to be Xavier Malate, and while a nun was changing him, handling him like a baby, he was tittering and explaining that they wouldn't get him to die out of turn.

"Augustin first!" he said with a wink.

CHAPTER 5

WITHOUT NEEDING TO OPEN HIS EYES HE KNEW it was still night, and that the little flat lamp was shedding a faint light in one corner of the room, like a tiny moon. He also knew that something unusual was happening, though he couldn't have said what, something missing, a *lack*, rather than something too much, and when he had roused up sufficiently he realized that what had disturbed him was the silence surrounding the house after the storm that had been raging for days, as though all at once the universe had ceased to vibrate.

There was a ray of light under the door into the study, he could see it through the tiny slit between his eyelids. To see the time by his alarm clock he would have to turn his head, and he didn't feel like moving.

He listened. There was someone moving in the next room, without excessive caution, not furtively, and he recognized the sound of logs being dumped on the hearth and the familiar crackle of the kindling. When the smell of the burning wood began to reach his nostrils, not before, he called out:

"Emile!"

The chauffeur opened the door; he had not yet shaved or put on his white jacket, and the sleepless night had clouded his eyes.

"Did you call, sir?"

"What time is it?"

"A few minutes past five. It suddenly turned cold, late in the night, and now it feels like frost. So I'm starting the fire. Did I wake you?"

"No."

After a short silence, Emile remarked:

"So you see, nobody came, after all."

The old man repeated:

"Nobody came, you're right."

"Would you like your tea right away?"

From his bed he could watch the flames leaping in the study fireplace.

"Yes, please."

Then, as Emile reached the door, he called him back:

"Open the shutters first, if you don't mind."

Just as, in the evening, he liked to cloak himself in solitude, in the morning he was eager to resume contact with life, eager in an anxious, almost frightened way.

Day was still far off, there was no sign of dawn, and yet the night was not black but white, and a light, pale-colored vapor, which was actually fog, had time to float into the room while Emile leaned out to push back the shutters.

"The cold's as sharp as midwinter, and later on, with this damp rising as though the ground were a sponge, we shan't be able to see as far as the garden gate."

During this brief contact with the outer world they had heard the foghorn wailing, muted, in the distance. At some point during the night the wind had fallen to a flat calm, but ordinary life, in abeyance during the tempest of the last few days, had not yet got under way again and the countryside still lay, as it were, in limbo.

"I'll bring your tea in five minutes."

Coffee had been forbidden, and now he was only allowed weak tea. Of all the privations he had to endure, this was the only one he found painful, and he sometimes went into the kitchen, while Gabrielle was getting breakfast for the staff, just for a whiff of the coffee they were to drink.

Chalamont hadn't come, but it was too soon to think about that, nothing definite being known as yet. But not to have received the visit he had regarded as almost certain was a disappointment, though still vague and unacknowledged. He felt ill at ease, anxious, as though he, too, suddenly lacked something, as though there were something missing in life.

Sitting up in bed, he drank his tea, while Emile prepared his linen and his suit, for he was always fully dressed first thing in the morning, and very few people could boast of having seen him with his toilet incomplete. Even a dressing gown, he considered, belonged to the privacy of the bedroom, and he never wore one in his study.

On his way to take a shower—he had had to give up baths—he glanced out of the window and saw the glowing tip of a cigarette close to the house.

"Is that still Aillevard?"

"No. Rougé took over from him just before two o'clock, about the time when the weather changed, and I gave him a cup of coffee a while ago."

The house was starting to stir again. There was a light in Gabrielle's room—she'd be coming down to start her fire—and in Milleran's as well. Water was running through a pipe. A cow mooed in the nearest barn and another answered it from farther off, more faintly. While the storm lasted not a cow had been heard.

He took his shower, tepid and very short, as he had been

advised, after which Emile helped him to dry himself and get into his clothes. Emile smelled strongly of cold cigarette, especially in the early morning. It made the Premier feel queasy, but he didn't like to ask the man to stop smoking.

"If you don't need me I'll go up quickly to change and shave."

Usually this, too, was an hour he enjoyed. In summer it was already light and he could see children taking cattle to pasture in the fields along the cliff-top. Closer to him the house would be gradually waking up and he would stroll about idly, without impatience, in the four low-ceilinged rooms, going from one shelf to another, pausing, moving on, halting on the threshold to sniff the smell of damp soil and grass which, only quite recently, had gone back to being the same as in his childhood.

In autumn and winter he watched the slow dawn breaking, and there was nearly always a thin mist rising from the ground, in a sheet of unequal density, pierced with holes through which one sometimes glimpsed the church belfry.

Today the dawn was colorless, sketched with white gouache and charcoal, and only the whiter glow of the thickening fog showed that the light was strengthening.

The others were in the kitchen, eating. The tree near the front door was growing visible in misty outline, with its trunk that leaned eastward because of the sea wind and its leafless branches which all stretched eastward too; then the dim, ghostly figure of the policeman on guard came into view beside it. He seemed very far away, in another world, and even his footsteps were inaudible, as though the fog was muffling sounds as well as blurring forms.

Now and again the Premier looked at the time, then at

the little white radio set on his desk. Before the moment had come to switch it on, he saw young Marie advancing through the fog, growing gradually taller and clearer, her red jersey striking the only note of color in the landscape.

Tiny drops of moisture must be clinging to her untidy hair, as they did to every blade of grass she walked over. When she noisily opened the kitchen door, exclamations could be heard, laughter from Emile. Her mother must have had the baby, but he didn't call her to make sure.

He was counting the minutes now, and he turned on the radio too soon, had to put up with a stupid popular song followed by the whole of the weather report, to which he paid no attention. Thursday, November 4th. Feast of St. Charles. Paris market prices. Fruit and vegetables....

"*And here is our first news bulletin. Home news. Paris. As we anticipated yesterday evening, there was considerable activity all night in the Boulevard Suchet, where Monsieur Philippe Chalamont, entrusted by the President of the Republic with the task of forming a Cabinet on a multi-party basis, was visited by a number of prominent politicians belonging to various parties. Leaving the Deputy for the sixteenth arrondissement's flat at about four o'clock this morning, Monsieur Ernest Grouchard, leader of the Radical Party, whose visit had immediately succeeded that of the leader of the Socialist group, declared his satisfaction at the way the negotiations were proceeding. It is thought that Monsieur Chalamont will go to the Elysée fairly early in the morning, to give the Head of the State his definite reply, as promised. Marseilles. The* Mélina, *a liner belonging to the Messageries Maritimes, on board which ...*"

He switched off, without noticing that Milleran had come into the study. His reaction was a gloomy amazement, a sensation of emptiness not unlike what he had felt earlier when the noise of the storm had suddenly given out.

He had been waiting for Chalamont, almost certain he would come. Had he been secretly hoping for the visit? He didn't know. He didn't want to know, especially not just now.

While he had been imagining his former subordinate driving through the rain and wind, and had even gone so far as to think he might have had a breakdown on the way, Chalamont had been in his flat in the Boulevard Suchet, coldly playing the game, receiving the political leaders, one by one.

It was so unexpected, so monstrous, that he could not shake off his stupefaction, and at one moment he put the tip of his first finger to the corner of his eye, which was slightly moist.

Realizing that his secretary was standing in front of him, he asked her, as though collecting his thoughts from a great distance and resentful of her intrusion:

"What is it?"

"I wanted to ask whether I should ring up Evreux tight away."

He took a little time to remember, while Milleran went on:

"A hospital is open night and day, so perhaps there's no need to wait till nine o'clock?"

He still sat sluggishly in his armchair, and his set, vacant stare began to worry Milleran, though she knew from experience that she must pretend not to notice it. Simply to break the silence, she announced:

"Young Marie has a little sister. That's the fifth girl in the family."

"Leave me alone for a while, if you don't mind."

"May I go into my office?"

"No. Somewhere else. Wherever you like."

There remained one explanation, on which he pinned his hopes: that Chalamont's confession had vanished. To check this theory, he was sending Milleran away, and as soon as she was in the kitchen he went to the farthest bookcase and, with a feverish hand, pulled out *Le Roi Pausole* in its heavy cardboard case.

At that moment he was hoping . . .

But the second folder opened of its own accord at page 40, and there lay the sheet of paper with the heading of the Premier's office, ironical, looking no more important than an old love letter or a four-leaf clover forgotten between the pages of a book. And indeed it was of very slight importance, despite its dramatic statement and the care he had taken of it, for it had not prevented anything.

"*I, the undersigned, Philippe Chalamont . . .* "

With a gesture of impatience such as he had rarely indulged in during his life, and of which he was at once ashamed, he hurled the book to the ground, so that he suffered the humiliation of being obliged to get down and pick up the scattered parts, the loose engravings, the original drawings.

Because of his ex-secretary, he was reduced to watching the door, for fear someone might suddenly come in and find him on all fours on the floor. And he'd look even more ridiculous if his leg suddenly played him one of its tricks while he was in this position!

Milleran waited in the kitchen, unaware of what was going on, listening hard, and it was at least ten minutes before the bell recalled her to the study.

The Premier had gone back to the Louis-Philippe

armchair. His strained manner had disappeared, replaced by a calm that she found uncomfortable because it was obviously artificial, like his voice, which had an unaccustomed, unnaturally suave note when he said:

"You may telephone now."

He cared nothing for Malate just then, but it was important for life to go on as usual, for the little everyday events to follow one another in the expected order. That was a kind of moral hygiene and the only way of keeping a cool head.

If the paper had disappeared from the Pierre Louÿs book he would have understood Chalamont's behavior, accepted it, perhaps even approved it, and it would not have affected him personally.

With the document still in his hands, things were different. That meant that his former secretary had reached the cynical conclusion that the way lay open, that the obstacle that had delayed him on his way up the political ladder had in his opinion ceased to exist.

The old man was still living, of course, on the top of some cliff in Normandy, but the scrap of paper he had brandished for so long had lost its value as a scarecrow, just as the ink of the writing on it was fading.

Chalamont was behaving as though the Premier were dead.

He had made his decision during the night, with his eyes open, knowing what he was about, weighing the risks, foreseeing every eventuality.

It had not occurred to him to call up. The breakdown had nothing to do with his silence. He had not set out for Les Ebergues, had sent nobody, this time, to plead his cause or negotiate on his behalf.

"Hello? Is that Evreux hospital?"

Was the Premier really going to bother about that maniac who had been haunting him for so many years? Had he come down to that? He was tempted to rush into the next room, take the telephone away from his secretary and ring off. Everything was annoying him, including the fog, too motionless and stupid, which was pressing against the window and making the outside world look unearthly.

"Yes . . . You say he's . . . I can't quite hear you, mademoiselle . . . Yes . . . Yes . . . That's better . . . You didn't know how long he's been there? . . . I understand . . . I shall probably ring you again later . . . Thank you. . . . "

"Well, so what?" he snarled, when Milleran came in, looking embarrassed.

"Dr. Jaquemont, or Jeaumont, I couldn't get the name clearly, is operating on him now. . . . He went into the theater at a quarter past seven. . . . They expect it to take a long time. . . . It seems that . . . "

"Why did you say you'd call back?"

"I don't know . . . I thought you'd want to know."

He grunted:

"You aren't here to think!"

It was all too idiotic. Here he was, worrying about the fate of a man who meant nothing to him, who ought to be shut up in a lunatic asylum, for no earthly reason except that the fellow had been assuring him for forty years:

"I'll be at your funeral."

Now it was Malate who was on the operating table, at the age of eighty-three—for he was a year older than his former schoolfellow—with a cancer of the throat that two previous operations had done nothing to cure. Whether he died or whether he didn't, what difference would it make? What did it matter?

"Tell Emile to take the car and go to Etretat for the papers."

"I think the barber's arriving," she announced, looking out of the window and seeing a man on a bicycle, distorted by the fog to an apocalyptic monster.

"Let him come in, then."

The barber, Fernand Bavet, who was also a saddler, came every morning to shave him, for the Premier was among the survivors of a period when men did not shave themselves, and he had always refused to do it, just as he had refused to learn to drive a car.

Bavet was a florid, full-blooded man with a throaty voice.

"Well, sir, what do you think of this pea souper? One can't see three yards in front of one's nose, and I nearly ran into one of your guardian angels ..."

Most barbers' hands smell of cigarette smoke, which is unpleasant enough. Bavet's smelled of fresh leather as well, of newly slaughtered animals, and his breath stank of calvados.

As the Premier grew older he became more sensitive to smells, and was disgusted by things he never noticed in the old days, as though his body, as it dried up, was being purified by a kind of disincarnation.

"Now tell me, you who're in the know, are we going to have a government, after all?"

Bavet's good humor met with no response and he lapsed into resigned silence, a little vexed, all the same, for he was fond of telling his cafe cronies:

"The old man? I shave him every day and with me he's just like anybody else, I speak as straight to him as I would to one of you. ..."

Still, everybody has good days and bad ones, haven't they? His job finished, the barber put away his instruments, bowed to his customer, and went off to the kitchen, where Gabrielle always gave him a drink. The engine of the car was running; Emile was warming it up before starting out to fetch the papers from Etretat, since the grocer's at Bénouville only took one local daily, printed at Le Havre, and two or three Paris papers which arrived very late.

A three-minute news bulletin was being broadcast every hour, and at nine o'clock the Premier listened again, but only to hear a repetition of what he knew already.

Thereupon, turning to Milleran, who was opening the letters, he inquired, so impatiently that she jumped:

"Well? Aren't you going to call up Evreux?"

"I'm very sorry...."

She hadn't dared, not quite knowing, as things were, what she should do and what she shouldn't.

"Get me Evreux, mademoiselle.... Yes, the same number as before.... A priority call, yes...."

For each successive government had had the courtesy to leave him the right to priority over the telephone, as though he were still in office. Would that favor continue under a Chalamont government?

Why did the day still seem so empty? It was no different from any other, and yet he felt as though he were going round and round in space, like a fish in a bowl, opening and shutting his mouth soundlessly, just like one.

On other days the hours were never too long. In a few minutes, when she had finished opening the envelopes and setting aside bills, prospectuses, and the invitations some people persisted in sending him, Milleran would bring him the letters to read, and usually he enjoyed this; there was an element of surprise that he appreciated, and it didn't bore him to say what answers should be sent, or to dictate a few letters when he thought it worth while.

In the last few days he hadn't cursed the storm, which ought to have annoyed him, but now he was glowering at the foggy scene outside as though suspecting that nature was perfidiously scheming to smother him.

He felt some difficulty in breathing. In a quarter of an hour Madame Blanche would arrive to give him his injection, and because of yesterday's outing, which she had tried to prevent, and his two sneezes, which she hadn't failed to notice, she would watch him distrustfully, suspecting that he was concealing something from her.

He couldn't stand women who looked at one as though one were a child caught telling a fib. Madame Blanche had threatened him with a cold, and she'd be watching for the symptoms of a cold. Wasn't it often from a cold that old people died when they had no other illness?

"Hello? Yes ... What did you say? ... No, don't disturb him. ... Thank you, mademoiselle."

"Disturb whom?"

"The surgeon."

"Why?"

"I was talking to the matron and she thought you might want to hear details. ... "

"Details of what?"

Before she had time to reply, he went on sharply:

"He's dead, isn't that it?"

"Yes ... During the operation ... "

With a rudeness in which he seldom indulged, he exclaimed:

"What the hell do you suppose I care about that? Wait!

Send a line to the director of the hospital to say they're not to chuck him into a pauper's grave. He's to have a decent funeral, but no more. Ask what it will cost and make out a check for me to sign."

Did he feel relieved that Xavier Malate should have been the first to go, in spite of his bragging? His old schoolfellow had been mistaken. He'd clung to life for no purpose. His last chance now was for their two funerals to take place on the same day, and the Premier was determined that shouldn't happen.

There was only one person left now who had known the Rue Saint-Louis in his time, the little redheaded girl of those days. Was she going to die too, and leave him to be the last?

For quite a long time, on his way to the *lycée*, he used to gaze with an agreeable agitation at the chalky-white sign with its black letters, including an N written backwards, which composed the words: "Ernest Archambault, Ironmonger." There was no actual shop. From the front the house looked just like others in the district, with lace-curtained windows and ferns in copper pots. At the end of a dank alleyway one could see the yard and a glass-roofed workshop from which the clang of hammers emerged, audible as far as the *lycée*.

In the classroom Xavier Malate had sat two rows away from him, near the stove, which it was his privilege to stoke up. Between them sat a boy who was taller than the others, better dressed, with a rather affected manner, who lived in a château outside the town and sometimes came to school on horseback, wearing riding boots, carrying a crop, and followed by a servant mounted on a heavier animal. He was a Count, whose name he had forgotten like so many others.

Who was the present occupant of the house where he

had been born and lived until he was seventeen? Had it been pulled down? In his time the bricks had been almost black, there had been a green-painted door and a brass plate announcing his father's surgery hours.

He still had, put away somewhere, a box full of old photos he'd always meant to sort out. There was one of his father, who'd had a sandy mustache and a little pointed beard like Henri III, and he could still remember how he had smelled of sour wine.

He had scarcely known his mother, for she had died when he was five and was still, apparently, a chubby little boy as fat as butter. An aunt had arrived from the country to look after him and his elder sister, and later on his sister, still almost a child, with short skirts and pigtails, had run the house with the help of one maid, who for some mysterious reason was always changing.

In actual fact nobody had brought him up. He had brought himself up. He could still recall the names of certain streets which had perhaps influenced his career.

The Rue Dupont-de-l'Eure, for instance. He even remembered the dates, for he had always had a memory for figures, including, later on, telephone numbers. *1767–1855. Patriot. Politician renowned for his integrity.*

Rue Bayet (1760–1794).

A patriot, too, and a Girondist Deputy during the Revolution.

But it was not on the scaffold that he had died at the age of thirty-four. He had committed suicide at Bordeaux, which he had chosen as his exile after being deserted by his party.

Rue Jules-Janin. Writer and critic, Member of the Académie Française . . .

At the age of fifteen, because of Janin, he had dreamed of the Académie Française, and had almost chosen literature as his career.

Rue Gambetta (1838–1882) ...

Come to think of it, he might have met Gambetta if he'd lived in Paris instead of at Evreux.

Rue Jean-Jaurès (1859–1914) ...

As a schoolboy he hadn't known that one day he would sit in the Chamber as Jaurès' colleague and would witness his assassination.

He didn't admit it in his memoirs, not even in the secret ones: but right from boyhood he had known he, too, would one day have his street, even his statue in public places.

In those days he had felt nothing more than pitying condescension for his father, who spent his time, day and night, in all weathers, hastening from one patient to another, carrying his heavy, shapeless bag of instruments, or in his office, with its frosted glass windows, seeing an endless stream of poor patients who filled the waiting room to overflowing and were often to be found sitting on the stairs.

He resented, as a piece of humbug, the way his father carried in practice although he didn't believe in medicine, and it was not until much later, after his father's death, that he began to reflect on something he'd been fond of saying:

"I do my patients as much good as other doctors, who believe in their vocation, and I run less risk of doing them harm."

So his father had not been the uncouth, slightly bohemian, rather drunken fellow that he had imagined, in whom, as a child, he had refused to take any interest.

At the age of twenty he had returned to Evreux for his sister's marriage to one of the clerks at the Town Hall. Had he seen her three times after that, before she died of peritonitis when she was getting on toward seventy? He hadn't gone to her funeral, and he seemed to remember that he'd been on an official visit to South America at the time. He had nephews and nieces with children of their own, but he'd never felt any desire to get to know them.

Why had Milleran rushed off to the kitchen as soon as she had seen Madame Blanche approaching the house? To tell her he didn't seem quite himself, or that Xavier Malate's death had upset him?

In the first place, it wasn't true. And in the second place, as he always said, he loathed the sidelong glances they gave him, as though they were constantly expecting . . .

Expecting what?

When the nurse came in, carrying the little bowl with the syringe, he looked her straight in the eye and forestalled her inquiries by declaring:

"I feel perfectly fit and I haven't a cold. Give me my injection quickly and leave me in peace."

It cost him an effort every morning, in his bedroom, the door of which she always closed behind her, to let down his trousers in front of her eyes and expose his livid thigh.

"The left side today . . . "

Left and right, on alternate days.

"Have you taken your temperature?"

"I have not, and I don't intend to."

The telephone rang. Milleran knocked on the door; nothing in the world would have induced her to open it, for she knew the reception she would get.

"What is it?"

"A journalist who insists on speaking to you. . . . "

"Tell him I'm busy."

"He says you'll remember his name...."

"What is his name?"

"Loubat."

It was the squeaky-voiced reporter who had thrown Chalamont off his stride the previous evening, in the courtyard of the Elysée, by asking whether he meant to spend the night on the road.

"What am I to tell him?"

"That I have nothing to say."

Madame Blanche was asking:

"Did I hurt you?"

"No."

It was no business of hers. Having pulled up his trousers he opened the door, to hear his secretary saying into the telephone:

"I assure you I did tell him.... No ... I can't ... You don't know him ... What?"

Feeling his presence behind her, she started.

"What does he want?"

"Just a minute, please," she said again into the telephone.

Then, putting her hand over the mouthpiece, she explained:

"He insists on my asking you a question."

"What question?"

"Whether it's true that you and Chalamont are reconciled."

She spoke again into the mouthpiece:

"Just a moment.... No.... I asked you to hold on...."

The Premier stood motionless, as though wondering what line to take, and all at once he grabbed the receiver and rapped out, before hanging up with a jerk:

"Go and ask him yourself. I wish you good day."

Then, turning to Milleran, he inquired, in a voice almost as disagreeable as the journalist's:

"Do you know why he rang up this morning?"

"No."

"To make sure I was still alive."

She tried to laugh, as though he were joking.

"I mean it!"

"But ..."

"I know what I am taking about, *Mademoiselle* Milleran."

It was only on particular occasions that he addressed her in that way, with sarcastic emphasis. He went on, enunciating each syllable separately:

"For him, this morning, I ought logically to be dead. And he has expert knowledge!"

What did it matter whether she understood or not! He was not talking to her but to himself, or perhaps to History, and what he said was the literal truth.

If he were alive, really alive, it would be unthinkable for Chalamont ...

"Turn on the radio, please. It's ten o'clock. The President will be beginning his audiences at the Elysée. You'll see!"

She didn't know what she was to see. Bewildered, she was looking anxiously at Madame Blanche, who was going off to the kitchen with her battered bowl.

"*At the fourth pip it will be ...*"

He had picked up the little clock and was putting it exactly right.

"*And here is the latest news. We have just been informed that Monsieur Philippe Chalamont, who was called to the Elysée yesterday afternoon, has paid a second visit to the President of the Republic. He has officially undertaken to form a Cabinet on a wide coalition basis, whose main lines*

*are already known, and it is hoped, in well-informed circles,
that the list of Ministers will be announced before the end of
the afternoon....*"

She didn't know whether to switch off or not.

"Leave it, for heaven's sake. Don't you understand it's not
finished yet?"

He was right. After a pause, a crackling of paper, the announcer began again:

"*A few names have already been mentioned ...*"

She was watching him as, pale and tense, with angry
eyes, he glared at her and at the radio set, as though ready to
burst into rage at any moment.

"*... Monsieur Etienne Blanche, Radical Socialist, is expected to be the Keeper of the Seals ...*"

An old hand who'd been in two of the Premier's Cabinets, once at the Board of Trade and once, already, at the
Ministry of Justice.

"*... Monsieur Jean-Louis Lajoux, Secretary of the Socialist Party, Minister of State ...*"

He had been starting his career when the Premier left
the scene, and though he vaguely remembered him, it was
only as a background figure.

"*... Ferdinand Jusset, another Socialist ...*"

Another old hand, about whom there was a note, slipped
into a volume of La Bruyère.

"*And then Monsieur Vabre, Monsieur Montois, and ...*"

"That'll do!" he said curtly.

He very nearly added:

"Get me Paris on the telephone...."

There were at least ten numbers on the tip of his tongue,
he knew them by heart, and he need only ring one of them
in order to sink the Ministry that was being formed.

He was on the point of doing it, and the effort to contain himself, remain worthy of himself, was so great that he felt an attack coming on. His fingers, his knees began to shake, and as usual at such moments his nerves refused to obey him; the mechanism suddenly began to race at increasing speed.

Without a word he went hastily into his bedroom, hoping Milleran had not noticed anything and wouldn't go and fetch Madame Blanche. With feverish haste he snatched out of a drawer two sedative pills, prescribed for him to take at such moments.

In ten minutes, at most, the drug would take effect and he would relax, gradually becoming languid and a little vague, as though after a sleepless night.

Meanwhile he stood leaning against the wall, near the square window with its small panes, watching young Marie as, in her red jersey, she stood in the fog, more translucent now, but still thick, hanging out washing on a line slung between two apple trees.

He was tempted to open the window and call to her, say no matter what, for it was too stupid to expect washing to dry in this sodden atmosphere.

But why interfere? It didn't concern him.

Was there anything left that did concern him?

All he had to do was to wait, trying to keep as calm as possible, until the drug took effect.

Even Emile wasn't back from Etretat, where Gabrielle must have given him a whole lot of errands.

"Hush! . . . One . . . two . . . three . . . four . . . "

Standing motionless, he was counting his pulse, as though his life were still of importance.

CHAPTER 6

THE INSTRUCTIONS GIVEN BY GAFFÉ AND DR. Lalinde, with the approval of Professor Fumet, were to take one pill, not two, at a moment of crisis, and another three hours later if need be. He had deliberately doubled the dose, partly because he was in a hurry to calm his panic-stricken nerves, but chiefly as a protest, in defiance.

The result was that before the usual ten minutes were up he began to see black spots before his eyes, flickering so that he felt dizzy, and that once seated in his armchair, in which he had hastily taken refuge, he felt torpor creeping over him.

If he had been an ordinary man he would have surrendered to it with relief, but they wouldn't let him. At the slightest change in his habits or behavior they would begin by summoning the young doctor from Le Havre, who in his turn would send for the man from Rouen, and once they were together the pair would shift the responsibility to Fumet, by telephone.

Did Fumet, in his turn, report to somebody higher up, while the three police inspectors were informing their own boss of the Premier's off moments, as though he were a kind of sacred animal?

The idea made him cross, illogically, for a few minutes

earlier he had been moping about being forgotten in Paris, almost in a rage because somebody was ignoring his veto.

When Milleran came in with the letters she had sorted, he was looking surly, his small eyes were tired but aggressive, and as she was about to put down the letters on his desk he stopped her with a gesture.

"Read them to me."

He had not the energy to read them himself, for his eyelids were heavy and his brain dulled.

He began by asking:

"Where's Madame Blanche?"

"In the waiting room."

This was the name given to the library farthest from his bedroom, the one that led to the front hall and was, indeed, used as a waiting room when necessary. If Madame Blanche was settled there, with a book or some magazines, it was because she wasn't pleased with the state she had found him in and expected him to be needing her, unless it was Milleran who had said something to her.

What was the use of bothering about it, mulling over the same old suspicions and resentments? He said again, resignedly:

"Read them to me."

The public believed that he had a great deal of correspondence, as he used to when he was Premier, but in actual fact the postman usually brought a mere handful of letters every morning, except on the days following the publication of an article about him in some magazine or newspaper with a big circulation.

From time to time somebody would come bothering him for this purpose, from one country or another, invariably asking the same questions and taking the same photos, and he knew so well where they would ask him to stand that he would get into position even before the photographer opened his mouth.

The resulting correspondence was almost identical each time. He would be asked for his autograph, often on cards specially cut to be filed in a collection, or on postcard photographs of himself such as were on sale in stationers' shops.

From Oslo a girl of sixteen, writing poor French in a careful hand, sent him a list of questions, with blank spaces for the answers, explaining that her teacher had asked her to write an essay of not less than six pages on the Premier's career.

The questions began like those on a passport application form:

"*Place of birth*:

"*Date of birth*:

"*Education*:"

She could have found those particulars in any encyclopedia, even in her own country.

"*What made you choose politics as your career?*

"*Which statesman did you admire most when you began your career?*

"*Did you hold certain theories when you were very young, and have any of them altered as time went on?*

"*If so, why?*

"*What recreations have you gone in for?*

"*Which of them do you still keep up?*

"*Are you satisfied with your life?*"

Milleran had been surprised when he had sent a serious reply to the girl, who in a few years would doubtless have settled down as a wife and mother.

An old couple—younger than he was, though!—

ingenuously requested him to help them end their days in the way they had always dreamed of, by making them a present of a cottage in the country, not too far from Bergerac, where the husband had just been pensioned off from his job as a postman.

A lot of people supposed him to be rich. Humble people wouldn't have understood how a man who had led the country so often and for such long periods, living in palatial government houses and surrounded by official pomp, could be left with no private fortune at the age of eighty-two.

Yet so it was, and the Chamber had voted him a pension without his asking for it. The government also paid Madame Blanche's salary and, since he had left Paris, Emile's wages.

Were they afraid it might be said later on that France had left one of her great men to die in poverty?

So even at Les Ebergues, after retiring from public life, he was not completely independent, he remained a kind of civil servant.

"After all, there are funds for preserving historic monuments!" he sometimes said jokingly.

At other times he would point out that owners of premises classed as of historic interest were forbidden by law to make the slightest structural alteration in them. Didn't he come under the same heading? Had he any right to reveal himself in a light different from that in which the history books displayed him?

The care taken in this respect was such that three policemen took turns outside his door, and he felt convinced that his telephone was regularly tapped, his correspondence, especially letters from well-known foreigners, opened before being sent on to him. Or did Milleran take it upon herself

to report to the authorities about what he wrote and whom
he saw?

"*Dear Sir,*

"*I am at present writing a large-scale work on a man with
whom: you were well acquainted, and venture . . .* "

He was not jealous, although there were many letters
of that kind. For some twenty years there had been five of
them, known as the Grand Old Men, each representing his
own country more or less uninterruptedly, and between
them they had controlled world policy.

They used to meet periodically, on one continent or
another, nearly always in some well-known spa, for conferences to which journalists and photographers would flock
in hundreds.

The slightest word uttered by one of them, the faint-
est frown on emerging from a meeting, would be reported
in press communiqués with banner headlines in all the
newspapers.

Sometimes they had quarrels, followed by spectacular
reconciliations, often staged merely for their own amusement; some of their talks, whose outcome the world awaited
in breathless suspense, had turned only on trivial subjects.

The Englishman, who in private was the most humorous
and cynical of the five, would look at his watch on arriving.

"How long are we supposed to argue before agreeing on
this communiqué?"

And he would produce from his pocket a ready-drafted
announcement.

"If only they were decent enough to leave us some cards,
we could have a game of bridge. . . . "

They all belonged to the same generation, except the
American, who had died young, at sixty-seven, before any

of the others. They had summed one another up so precisely that each knew the true worth of all the others, and even their little eccentricities.

"Gentlemen, with my country about to go to the polls, it is imperative for me today to put my foot in it, as our journalist friends will report presently. So we will announce that I banged on the table and that my obstinacy has brought the conference to a deadlock."

There was nearly always a garden surrounding the luxury hotels that were taken over on these occasions, and as soon as one of the five ventured into it he would be set upon by reporters and photographers.

All five were accustomed to power and fame, and yet the varying shares of publicity they received had now and then caused sulks and sub acid comments from one to another; these white-haired statesmen, depicted in profile on their countries' stamps, descended on such occasions to behaving like a bunch of actors.

In the margins of his book the Premier had noted some traits of this kind, not all of them, only the most typical, especially those with a certain human quality.

And now, when, except for Cornelio, who had lost his wits, he was the last survivor of the group, he still felt a slight twinge when somebody wrote to ask him for information about one of them, and not about himself!

In London, New York, Berlin, Stockholm, all over the world, people were still writing books about him and about the others, and he sometimes caught himself feeling tempted to make up the whole of each of them!

"I'll answer that tomorrow. Remind me. You may go on reading."

An unknown man wanted his help in obtaining a post in the prison administration.

"*I come from Evreux, like yourself, and when I was young my grandfather often talked to me about you, for you lived in the same street and he knew you well.* . . . "

Milleran was watching him furtively, wondering whether he had dozed off, but his white, smooth-skinned hand, which now had the unquestionable beauty of an inanimate object, signed to her to continue.

"*Dear Sir,*

"*I have applied everywhere, I have knocked on every door, and you are my last hope. The whole world acknowledges your benevolence and your deep understanding of human nature, and I am confident that you will understand me, you who* . . . "

A professional sponger.

"Next one!"

"That's all, sir."

"Didn't I have an appointment for today?"

"Yes, the Spanish general was coming, but he sent a message to say he's ill with influenza at San Sebastian. . . . "

Speaking of generals, there was one who seemed likely to outlive them all, arid of whom the Premier thought with some envy and a touch of annoyance. He was ninety-three years old, but he turned up every Thursday, alert and inclined to be waggish, at the meetings of the Académie Française, of which he was a member. A month ago there had been an article about him in a weekly paper, including a photo where he appeared in shorts, bare-chested, doing exercises in his garden under the indulgent eye of his wife, who sat on a bench in the background as though watching a child at play.

Was it really worth it?

At Evreux, at this very moment, someone was laying out Xavier Malate, whose worries were at an end. He was through with everything. And he, who had been haunted by the idea of burial, would have nobody to walk behind his hearse, unless some old maid automatically turned up to follow it, as occasionally happens.

For a long time the Premier had paid no attention to the deaths of people in his circle, most of whom were his elders. He considered they had had their day, even those who died at fifty.

Then, when men hardly older than himself began to die as well, he had sometimes felt a certain selfish satisfaction, if not downright pleasure.

Someone else had been taken, and he was spared!

But the ranks of his own generation had gradually thinned, the Five Grand Old Men had begun to drop out, and on each occasion nowadays he caught himself counting, without grief but feeling vaguely apprehensive, as though it began to occur to him that his turn might really come one day.

He had never attended funerals, except on the very rare occasions when he was obliged to represent the government of the day. He had avoided death chambers, every kind of ceremonial death watch, not because they depressed him, but because he considered that kind of pomp to be in bad taste.

He would simply send in his card, or have himself represented by a member of his staff, and to his staff, too, he left the task of drawing up letters or telegrams of sympathy.

But Xavier Malate's death today had made a different impression on him, though he couldn't say exactly in what way. The drug had slowed down his mental processes, as though he were half asleep, and his thoughts were at one remove from reality.

For instance, he kept seeing the face of an old woman with thin hair and very long teeth. Heaven knew what had conjured it up, and there was no reason why she should resemble Eveline Archambault, whom he hadn't seen since she was just a little girl.

All the same he felt certain it was she, as she looked nowadays, and her face wore a curiously sweet expression, tinged with silent reproach.

She had doubtless prayed all her life that he might find religion before he died, as though words said to a priest could make any difference to anything. Like him she was seated in an armchair, an old rug over her knees, and a kind of stale smell emanated from her.

In the end he realized that the rug was the one that used to be wrapped around his mother's legs in the last weeks of her life. But what about the rest?

But for the fear of seeming ridiculous, he would have told Milleran to ring up Evreux again, the Town Hall, for instance, to inquire about Eveline, to find out whether she was still alive, if she were ill, if she had all she wanted.

He felt tired. He knew it was the natural effect of the drug he'd taken, but it gave him a depressingly helpless sensation, and if he'd had the right, he would have gone to bed.

A neighbor's cow, escaped from the barn, was running around the orchard, knocking against the boughs of the apple trees, pursued by a little boy armed with a stick.

That little boy would still be living long after he himself was dead. All those around him would outlive him, as would most of the earth's present population.

Would Emile tell the truth about Les Ebergues, later on? Perhaps so, for he liked vulgar stories and people would give him bigger tips if he made them laugh.

He had not been the first to use the cliff-top farm as a country house; before him a lawyer from Rauen—dead too now!—used to bring his family there for the holidays. The Premier had only made the additions required for his own convenience, such as the tunnel that now linked what were originally two separate buildings.

Names were of no importance to him, so he had not altered the one the property went by when he bought it.

The local people had told him that the word "*éber-gues*" referred to portions of the codfish prepared for use as bait, and as Fécamp was a codfishers' port and fishing was the mainstay of the whole coast, he had been satisfied with that explanation. Probably the skipper of a fishing smack or the owner of a small fleet had lived in the house at one time?

But one day when Emile was tearing away the ivy that had crept over the parapet of an old well, he had brought to light an inscription, roughly cut in the stone:

Les Ebernes
1701

The Premier had happened to mention this to the schoolmaster, who was also Secretary of the District Council and sometimes came to borrow books from him. The schoolmaster had had the curiosity to look up the old land-survey maps, and had found the property marked on them by the same name as that on the well.

However, nobody could tell him what "*ébernes*" were,

until at last he found the explanation in the big *Littré* dictionary:

"*Eberner*: to wipe excrement off a child.

"*Eberneuses*: women who wipe excrement off children."

What kind of women had once lived in the house and been given the nickname that had stuck to the place afterwards? And what later and more prudish occupant had given that cunning twist to the spelling of the name?

He had mentioned that, too, in his secret memoirs, but would they ever be published? He was not sure whether he still wanted them to be. When the future of the country was at stake he had always been prompt to take the most fateful decisions, with no fear of committing an error, but, faced with the question of what he should reveal about his own life, he became hesitant and was tormented by scruples.

The picture the world had formed of him was cut and dried, it took no account of the changes wrought by time, it was rudimentary and often downright false, and his legend included one particular chapter he had always tried to correct, but in vain.

It had appeared in the scandalmongering rags of the day, and later in a national newspaper, under the heading: "A Gentleman and His Tailor."

For thirty years his opponents had made the most of it during every election campaign. Only the title had altered from time to time, the variants including "Tradesman's Entrance" and "The Countess's Chambermaid."

The chambermaid and the Countess, for they had been real people, were both dead now, but the "Gentleman," who was about the same age as the Premier, still survived and could be seen every afternoon at the races, upright as ever, but with creaky joints.

This was the notorious Créveaux case, which had kept the Premier out of several successive Cabinets, just as another man had been barred from office for ten years by a certain letter hidden between the pages of *Le Roi Pausole*.

The difference was that he himself had been innocent, at least of the charge brought against him. He was hardly more than forty, and had just joined a Cabinet for the first time— as Minister of Public Works, in which capacity he was about to be visited by Xavier Malate.

Wasn't it odd the way things linked up through time and space, wreathing together mockingly, as it were? Could it have been on the actual day of Xavier's visit that . . .

Anyway, that didn't matter. In those days Marthe de Créveaux, Marthe de C., as the spiteful columnists used to call her, held regular receptions in her private mansion in the Rue de la Faisanderie, where it was her ambition to bring together everybody who was anybody in Paris diplomatic and political circles, admitting no one else except a few writers, provided they were members or prospective members of the Académie Française.

At that time the new Minister had never set foot in her house, for he went about very little even in those days, and was regarded as an uncouth, solitary being, so that the caricaturists were beginning to depict him in the guise of a bear.

Was it this reputation that had impelled Marthe de Créveaux to get hold of him, or was it because shrewd observers were beginning to foretell that he would soon be someone to be reckoned with?

The only daughter of a rich Bordeaux merchant, she had acquired a title by marrying the Comte de Créveaux, and thus launched herself in society as well. After that, Créveaux had resumed his bachelor habits, and there were days when

Marthe, in her ground-floor dining room, was entertaining a covey of ministers and ambassadors at luncheon, while her husband, in the second-floor suite he called his bachelor flat, was surrounded by a gay bunch of actresses and dramatists.

The Minister of Public Works had not been more than twice to the house in the Rue de la Faisanderie before it was rumored that the Countess had taken him in hand, just as she had chosen to play Egeria to two or three political men before him. There was some truth in the rumor. She was familiar with a world of which the future Premier knew very little, and she had decided to polish him up.

Was she beautiful, as the newspapers declared? After hearing her talked about, one was surprised, on seeing her for the first time, to discover that she was a small, helpless-seeming woman, looking much younger than one had expected, with nothing forceful or self-willed in her manner.

Though she spent her whole time launching and protecting men she found interesting, each of them felt he wanted to protect her from the others and from herself.

He wasn't certain he'd ever been fooled. Frankly, he had known what he wanted in those days, and he'd known she could help him to get it. Besides, he was flattered at being selected, when he was no more than a promising beginner, and even the luxurious atmosphere of her house had played its part.

Within a fortnight people were growing accustomed to speaking of them in one breath, and whenever the Comte de Créveaux met the young Minister he would hold out his hand with ironical emphasis and exclaim:

"Our very dear friend ..."

Contrary to what had been supposed, and was still

believed by some people who claimed to be in the know, physical attraction had played very little part in their relationship, and though Marthe, whose sexual needs were small, had given it to be understood that they were passionately in love, they had very seldom been in bed together.

Her great idea was to give him lessons in social behavior, and she had even set about teaching him how to dress.

It was embarrassing to remember all this, at the age of eighty-two when one was living in a little house on the Normandy coast where death would be one of the next visitors.

Because of this memory and a few others, he would have refused to have his life over again, if it had been offered to him.

For weeks and months had he not studied the attitudes and the manner she taught him, which she declared to be those befitting the perfect statesman?

And he, whose style of dress was correct and restrained, but with no attempt at smartness, had finally yielded to Marthe's insistence and paid a visit to the most fashionable tailor of the day, in the Faubourg Saint-Honoré.

"He's the only possible man, darling, unless you go to London for your clothes. He's my husband's tailor, by the way."

Nowadays he wondered whether he wouldn't prefer to have some dishonorable action on his conscience, as Chalamont had, rather than such a humiliating memory.

He could see the tailor, patronizing and ironical, his own reflection in the mirror, with one coat sleeve not yet tacked in place....

Hadn't he believed it mattered, if only for a short time, and hadn't he gone to the point of changing the shape of his hats, the color of his ties and gloves?

He'd taken to riding in the Bois, too, very early each morning.

The people who addressed him as "Minister" had no suspicion that he was behaving like a boy in calf love. Furthermore, in Marthe de Créveaux's house there was a young woman who was to get very much into the news because of him, and her name was Juliette.

She acted as companion as well as lady's maid, for Marthe couldn't bear to be alone and had to have someone with her even when she went shopping or to have a dress tried on, with the car following her from door to door. It was Juliette, too, who kept the list of her appointments, reminded her about them, answered the telephone, paid for small purchases in shops.

She came of a good middle-class family, dressed in trim navy or black, and looked every inch the convent-educated girl.

Was she a nymphomaniac even in those days? Probably, and he had probably not been the first to discover the fact.

On various occasions she had been alone on the ground floor with the future Premier, while Marthe was getting dressed, and she had played her game so well that one fine day, tried beyond his strength, he had taken her, on a sofa in the drawing room.

It became a habit, a necessity, and for her there could be no pleasure without danger, which she deliberately carried to the furthest limit, devising the most perilous situations.

The inevitable happened: Marthe de Créveaux caught them, and wounded pride, instead of prompting her to keep the secret, led to a scene of tragicomic fury that brought all the servants running.

Thrown out of the house together with Juliette, the

Premier had had no choice but to take a room for her in a quiet hotel, for he couldn't take her to the Ministry and would not have her in his flat on the Quai Malaquais.

The next day a minor newspaper had given a fairly accurate description of the incident, in a few lines, winding up with what purported to be the Comtesse de Créveaux's comment:

"When I think that I knocked off the man's corners and even bought his clothes for him!"

Had she really said that? It was possible, the words sounded just like her. She had not foreseen that they were to dog him right through his career and add greatly to his difficulties.

For the journalists, delighted with the windfall, had made an investigation, and the result had been the famous "Gentleman and His Tailor" article.

It asserted that Marthe de C. had sent the young Minister to her husband's tailor, whose address was given, and that it was Créveaux who, in due course, had paid the bill.

As white-faced as Chalamont had been when he wrote that letter, the Minister of Public Works had seized the telephone, rung up the tailor. He could recall nothing more agonizing than his feelings as he had listened to the voice at the other end of the line.

It was true! The journalists had not made it up. The tailor, his voice polite but unruffled, offered his apologies: he had believed . . . he had thought . . .

"So you took me for a pimp?" he had shouted into the telephone.

"Oh, Minister, I assure you that . . . "

Ordinarily he waited to pay his tailor, like any other shopkeeper, till the bill was sent in. It was barely three months since he had been to the Faubourg Saint-Honoré, and he had felt no surprise at not hearing from the man. After all, didn't some firms, especially in the luxury trade, send in their accounts only once a year?

Did Marthe de Créveaux pay in this way for the clothes of every man she took under her wing? He had never known because he had never seen her again, though she had written to him "to get rid of a misunderstanding and make peace" when he had become Premier.

Her end had been sad, for she, who had been so feverishly active, was bedridden with paralysis for five years, and when at last she died she was so wasted that she weighed no more than an eight-year-old girl.

Juliette had not remained on the Minister's hands for long; she was taken over by a journalist who introduced her to the newspaper world, where she soon made good on her own merits.

She had interviewed her ex-lover on several occasions, and had never failed to be astonished because he took no advantage of his renewed opportunity, as most men on whom she made a professional call no doubt did.

Her death had been more sudden than that of her former mistress, but no less sensational, for she was among the passengers on board a plane that crashed in flames in Holland on its way to Stockholm.

As for himself, he had sent the tailor a check, of course, but hundreds of thousands of people were still convinced that ...

And after all, didn't it come to much the same thing?

He didn't like the man he had been in those days. He didn't like himself as a little boy or as an adolescent, for that matter.

And nowadays the play-acting of the Five Grand Old Men, the airs they had put on, seemed to him to have been ridiculous.

Was all his indulgence reserved for the old man he had grown into, who was gradually drying up, like the Countess, until he'd become nothing but parchment stretched over a skeleton, with a brain spinning emptily in his bony skull?

For what did he think about all day long, while people crept like mice about the great man whose slightest sneeze was turned into a drama?

About himself! Himself! Always about himself!

He prowled round and round himself, sometimes with satisfaction, but usually discontented and bitter.

He had already told his story once, his story as the public wanted to have it, and no mere marginal notes scribbled later on would suffice to show him in his true light.

It was all false, because it was all described from a false angle.

The corrective notes were also false, being nothing but a shot at countering the legend.

As for the real man, as he had been and as he now was . . .

He stared uncomprehendingly at Gabrielle, who was standing in front of him, perhaps forgetting that she came every day at this time to tell him the same thing:

"Lunch is ready, sir."

It was Gabrielle's privilege to make this announcement, and she would not have left young Marie to do it for anything in the world. But surely, at the age of seventy, she should have got beyond such childishness?

The fog pressing against the dining-room windows was so dense that it seemed almost like a snowy landscape beneath a heavy, unbroken, motionless expanse of cloud, such as one sometimes sees in winter, when earth and sky are indivisible.

Young Marie had at last replaced her red jersey by a black dress and a white apron. She had been taught to hold the old man's chair while he bent forward, and then give it a gentle push, and this frightened her; she was always afraid of taking too long and letting him sit down on nothing.

"It seems you have another little sister?"

"Yes, sir."

"Is your mother pleased?"

"I don't know."

What was the use? Why utter meaningless words? The menu was almost as monotonous as the evening one. Half a grapefruit, for the vitamins, followed by three ounces of grilled meat, which had to be cut up for him now that his false teeth had got so loose, two potatoes and some boiled greens. Dessert would be an apple, a pear, or a few grapes, of which he wasn't allowed to eat the skins.

Would Chalamont, in Paris, follow tradition by inviting his new colleagues to a fashionable restaurant, where the main lines of his Cabinet's policy would be laid down over dessert?

In his own day the choice had almost always been a private room at Foyot's, near the Senate, or at Lapérouse's,

Men who'd often been in the same team would be there, swapping memories of previous Cabinets, old stagers would invariably be offered the same inglorious posts, and there were nearly always some newcomers, still ignorant of the rites, who would keep an uneasy eye on the old-timers.

Even the voices, the clatter of forks and the tinkle of glasses seemed to have a special resonance at those luncheons, and the headwaiters, who knew all the guests, hurried around with conspiratorial smiles, playing their part in the distribution of portfolios.

Different, but no less typical, was the noise made by the reporters and press photographers lunching in the main restaurant on the ground floor, who were just as conscious as the group upstairs of their role in the day's events.

Those two hours, in point of fact, were the most agreeable in the life of a government. Later in the afternoon, after the Ministers had been presented at the Elysée and been photographed on the steps with the President in their midst, his face wearing the inevitable smile, the time came to draft the ministerial statement, and then the difficulties began, with endless wrangling about each word, each comma.

Each of them had family matters and practical problems to consider as well. Were they to move into the various Ministries without waiting for the vote of confidence in the Chamber? Would there be room for the children? What furniture of one's own should one take along, and what dresses would one's wife need for official receptions?

He had been through this experience on twenty-two occasions, his biographers had made the tally for him, and on eight of them he had been the central figure.

Today it was Chalamont's turn, and suddenly something unexpected happened: remembering the bustle in Foyot's dining rooms, the Premier tried to visualize his one-time subordinate in that setting; but although he had spent more time with that man than with anyone else, been in closer contact with him than with any other, he was surprised to find himself unable to recall his features.

Yet it was only two days since he'd seen his photograph in the papers. Chalamont had altered in the last ten years, as was to be expected. But his memory didn't even present

him with the Chalamont of ten years ago. It conjured up
a young man of twenty-five whose expression, though already determined, was anxious, to whom he remembered
saying at the time:

"You'll have to learn to control your feelings."

"I know, Chief. I assure you I'm trying hard."

He had always called him "Chief," adopting the term by
which a great surgeon or doctor is addressed by his juniors.
He was no sentimentalist. He was cold and cynical. All the
same his cheeks would sometimes flush, all of a sudden,
with a bright color that his usual pallor made all the more
remarkable.

Did Chalamont, too, look back over his life now and
then, or was he, at sixty, still too young for that? Would he
be willing to have his time over again, and if so . . .

The Premier remembered precisely in what circumstances his former secretary could not keep from blushing,
despite his self-control. It was whenever he felt, rightly or
wrongly, that someone was trying to make him feel small.

He had formed an opinion about his own character
which he believed to be accurate, and which may indeed
have been so. He clung to this, and at the least threat to his
self-confidence the blood would instantly rush to his head.

He never argued, never protested. He made no attempt
to retort, but maintained a cautious silence; yet his flaming
cheeks alone betrayed his feelings.

In the Premier's office in the Hôtel Matignon the blood
had not risen to his cheeks; on the contrary, it had seemed
to drain out of his whole body.

"Are you tired?" young Marie inquired, suddenly arriving from worlds away.

He looked at the hand he had just brushed across his

face, then he gazed around him, as though awaking from sleep. His plate was hardly touched.

"Perhaps I am," he confessed in an undertone, so as not to be heard in the kitchen.

He made as if to rise, whereupon young Marie rushed to pull out his chair, and he looked so bent and feeble that she took hold of his arm.

"Thank you . . . I'm not hungry any longer. . . . "

She didn't know whether to follow him or not. She watched him as he moved away, shoulders bowed, long arms dangling, while he went with a wavering step into the passage leading to his study. She must have thought he might be going to fall, for she held herself ready to leap after him.

But he didn't even need to lean against the wall, and when at last he disappeared young Marie shrugged her shoulders, turned to clear the table.

When she went back to the kitchen with the dishes and plates, Milleran asked anxiously:

"What's happening?"

"I don't know. I think he's gone to bed. He looks tired."

But the Premier was not in bed, and when Milleran tiptoed into the study she found him asleep, with half open-mouth, in the Louis-Philippe armchair. His lower lip was slightly pendulous, as though from great weariness, or disgust.

CHAPTER 7

THIS TIME HE REALLY HAD GONE TO SLEEP, FOR he didn't hear Madame Blanche come when Milleran fetched her, nor was he aware that she was standing beside him, watch in hand, feeling his pulse with a light finger. Neither did he know that she had telephoned to the doctor, in lowered tones, or that while she was about it Milleran sat on a chair facing him, gazing steadily at him with a grave, sad face.

Then the women signed to each other and Whispered together. Milleran made way for Madame Blanche and went to her office.

More than half an hour went by like this, in a silence broken only by the regular ticking of the little clock, and at last the sound of a motor was heard, and a car drew up. Emile had said something to somebody, his voice hushed, too.

There was a kind of impromptu ballet going on around him, for now Madame Blanche, in her turn, made way for Dr. Gaffé, who, after taking the patient's pulse again, sat down facing him, as erect and formal as in a waiting room.

At one moment Emile had come in and put a log back into the fire, and the Premier had had no suspicion of all these furtive comings and goings. Yet he would have sworn that he had all along been aware of sitting supine in his armchair, with his lips parted and his breath whistling through them.

Had there really been a temporary separation between his mind and his body, the latter sitting inert while the former, still agile, flew in circles like a bird, sometimes into unknown worlds, sometimes through a universe not far removed from reality?

How could he have known, for instance, that when the effort became too exhausting he knitted his bushy eyebrows, or that he occasionally groaned at his helplessness? Yet later on they confirmed his impression that he had frowned and groaned. So what about it?

His own conviction was that he had got far enough outside himself to return and take a look at the almost inert carcass which was beginning to seem alien to him, and for which he felt more revulsion than pity.

During those two hours he had seen a vast number of faces, and had gone in pursuit of some of them, wondering what they were doing at his bedside. Others were familiar, but all the same he couldn't understand how they got there, the presence of the stationmaster of a little town in southern France, for example, where he had spent a brief holiday several years in succession.

Why was he here today? The old man knew the stationmaster had died long ago. But that little girl, whose hair had been arranged in ringlets and tied with a wide tricolor ribbon so that she could present him with a bouquet? Did her being here mean that she was dead too?

That was what had been worrying him most, while Gaffé waited, watching him, not daring to light a cigarette. He was trying to disentangle those among all these people who were still alive and those who were already in the other world, and his impression was that the frontier between life and death was hard to trace, that perhaps, even, there wasn't one.

Was that the great secret? He knew that during those two hours, when he had been intensely alive despite his body's inertia, he had a dozen times been on the point of solving all problems.

What made the job so difficult and disheartening was that he could never remain for long on the same plane. Perhaps his mind was not nimble enough, or lacked balance. Or could it be a question of weight? Or of habit? He was going up and down, sometimes gradually, sometimes by leaps and bounds, coming out into different worlds, some of which were fairly close to what is called reality, fairly familiar, while others were so remote and unlike that neither people nor objects were recognizable.

He had seen Marthe de Créveaux again. But she wasn't at all as he remembered her. It was not only that, as the papers had said when she died, she weighed no more than a little girl, but she looked like one, she had a little girl's innocence, and she was stark naked.

At the same time he blamed himself for remembering her only in order to clear his conscience, not so much from the business of the tailor as from the affair of the Legion of Honor. For it wasn't true that he had never shown partiality. That was a legend he had built up, like the others, the legend of the upright, uncompromising politician, doing his duty without fear or favor.

All the same, he had given the Legion of Honor to one of Marthe's protégés, an obscure country squire whose only title to such distinction was his ownership of a pack of hounds.

And a few days later hadn't he given an official reception

to an African potentate who must be propitiated for degrading practical reasons, though his proper place was in prison?

He had never asked pardon of anyone, and he was not going to begin at his time of life. Who but himself had any right to judge him?

He went on struggling. Of the faces that approached, glancing at him as thronging passers-by, in a street, cast a glance at the victim of an accident and go on their way, most were vacant-eyed, and he kept trying to stop one and ask whether this were not a procession of the dead that he was witnessing.

If so he too must be dead. And yet not quite, for they refused to treat him as one of themselves.

What was he, then, following zigzag flight like some clumsy night bird?

Very well! If it was because of Chalamont that they were coldshouldering him, he would leave Chalamont in peace. He had understood. He'd understood long ago, even perhaps at the Hôtel Matignon, but he had refused to show pity then, because he believed he had no right to do so.

He hadn't shown himself any pity, either. Why should he have shown any to his assistant?

"Time to pay, gentlemen!"

A voice shouted the words, like the attendant in a cheap dance hall who calls out in the intervals:

"Pass along the money, please!"

Had he been indignant when Chalamont had informed him that, after careful consideration, he had decided that his career would benefit if he were to have an *established position*, in other words if he married a woman with enough money to enable him to live in some style?

He'd been so far from indignant that he had attended the wedding as one of the witnesses.

Everything derives from everything. Everything counts. Everything helps. Everything changes. There is no waste. The day the wedding took place, at Saint-Honoré-d'Eylau, the die was cast and the Premier ought to have known it.

The moment had come when Chalamont had been summoned to pay for his situation, to repay his wife and his father-in-law, failing which he would be *displaced* in their esteem. . . .

Just as Marthe de Créveaux's lover had had to bestow a decoration on a stag hunter.

All this was on the lowest level, where he kept returning and getting bogged down. But in the course of the two hours he had made other discoveries, explored regions where he felt so much a stranger that he was not even certain what he had seen there.

He had felt cold, and that, too, was an attested fact, for the doctor was to tell him, later, that he had shivered more than once. Now it was his meeting with his father and Xavier Malate that had made him feel cold. He couldn't remember where he had met them, or what had passed between them, but he had seen them, and what had particularly struck him was that they had seemed to be on such cordial terms.

He had not expected that. It bothered him. It upset all his notions of human values. And why did the two of them, who had nothing in common except the fact of being dead, look at him with one and the same expression? It wasn't pity. That word had been withdrawn from circulation. Neither was it indifference. It was—the expression was inaccurate and bombastic, but he couldn't find a better—it was a *sublime serenity*.

In his father's case that might be all right. He was willing to concede the point. But that Malate should be endowed with sublime serenity, merely because he had died under the surgeon's knife! . . .

He didn't know what would happen next, and wondered whether he was going to wake up in the Louis-Philippe armchair at Les Ebergues. He was not sure whether he wanted to, but all the same he felt a little anxious.

They had caught him unawares, giving him no time to prepare for his departure, and it seemed to him that he had a great many things to do, a lot of questions to settle.

It was a pain in his right arm that proved to him that he was still in the body, and he opened his eyes, to discover, without surprise, that facing him sat Dr. Gaffé, who felt called upon to give him an encouraging smile.

"Had a good sleep, sir?"

Night was falling, and the doctor, at last able to move, got up to turn on the light. Milleran stirred in her office next door, walked quietly out to the first room, doubtless to tell Madame Blanche that he was awake now.

"So you see," said the old man gravely, "it appears that I'm not dead."

Why did Gaffé think fit to protest at this, when he was expecting it to happen from one day to the next, and there was no reason why it shouldn't be today?

The Premier had not been joking, he had merely taken note of a fact.

"Did you suddenly feel unwell during luncheon?"

He almost began to put on his usual act, replying in ambiguous or boorish monosyllables. But why bother?

"For no sufficient reason I lost my temper, so I took two sedative pills."

"Two!" exclaimed the doctor, relieved.

"Two. Now the effect has worn off."

Except that he was left with a nasty taste in his mouth, stiff limbs.

"Let's see your blood pressure.... No! Don't get up ... Madame Blanche will help me to take your coat off...."

He submitted meekly and didn't ask about his blood pressure, the figure of which, for once, the doctor forgot, or preferred not, to tell him.

In addition to this, Gaffé paraded his stethoscope over his chest and back, with the dedicated air he took on at such times.

"Cough, please ... Again ... Good ... A deep breath ... "

He had never been so biddable, and neither the doctor nor Madame Blanche could guess why—neither could Milleran, pricking up her ears in the next-door room.

The truth was that in his secret heart he had decided that it was all over. He couldn't have said at what precise moment this feeling of detachment had come over him, but it must have been during the strange journey of exploration he had made while his carcass lolled motionless and he was temporarily released from it.

It hadn't been painful, much less agonizing: he felt rather like a bubble rising to the surface of the water all of a sudden, for no apparent reason, and bursting, to mingle with the atmosphere. An easy separation, bringing him a relief so great that he could have cried out in delight, like a child watching the ascent of a red balloon:

"Oh!"

He would have liked to joke with them, in gratitude for their attentiveness and all they were doing for him, but they wouldn't understand and would probably have thought he was lightheaded.

He had never been lightheaded. So he had no standard of comparison, but he felt convinced that never in his life had he been so rational as at present.

"I suppose," said Gaffé quietly, after a glance at Madame Blanche, "that if I asked you to go to bed you'd dislike the idea? Simply as a precaution, of course. You yourself admit that you've been under a strain just lately. . . . "

He had said nothing of the kind. Milleran must have told the doctor that, while he was supposed to be asleep . . .

"There's frost in the air. It's going to be a very cold night, and there's no doubt that twenty-four hours' rest in bed . . . "

He thought it over, as a straightforward suggestion, and responded with an equally straightforward one:

"Suppose we put it off till this evening?"

In point of fact he was tempted to do as Gaffé wanted, but he had something else to see to first. And both the doctor and Madame Blanche would doubtless have been astonished if they could have read his thoughts.

He was eager to get away from the lot of them, Milleran, Emile, Gabrielle, young Marie. He was tired. He'd done his share and now he was giving up. Had it been possible, he would have asked them to put him into clean pajamas and lay him down in his bed, close the shutters against the fog outside, put out the lights, except the tiny moonlike disk of the night light.

Then, with the sheets up to his chin, curled up in utter, self-contained silence, in a solitude broken only by his weakening pulse, he would ebb slowly away, a little melancholy but quite without bitterness, and very rapidly, released both from shame and pride, he would settle his last accounts.

"*I beg your pardon . . .*"

Whose? That, as he had discovered, did not matter. There was no need of any name.

"*I did my best, with all the strength of a man and all a man's weaknesses. . . .*"

Would he see around him the attentive faces of Xavier Malate, Philippe Chalamont, his father, and others as well, those of Eveline Archambault, Marthe, the stationmaster, and the little girl with the bouquet?

"*I realize it's nothing to be proud of. . . .*"

They gave him no encouragement. He didn't need encouragement. He was all alone. The others had been merely witnesses, and he had learned that witnesses have no right to set up as judges. Neither had he. No one had. . . .

"*Forgive me. . . .*"

No sound of any kind, except the blood still pumping jerkily through his veins, and a crackling of logs in the next room.

He would keep his eyes open to the very last.

CHAPTER 8

"MADAME BLANCHE, WOULD YOU MIND GOING to the kitchen and waiting until I call? I have things to see to with Milleran. I promise not to take long, and not to get excited."

Gaffé had granted him his respite and given him an injection to pep him up, saying he would come back about seven o'clock.

"To be quite frank, as you've always asked me to be with you," he had said, "there's a slight wheezing sound in your bronchial tubes. But I don't think it's anything to worry about, for your temperature and pulse don't suggest there's any infection so far."

They were not accustomed to finding him so meek, and it made them uneasy, but what could he do to avoid worrying them? Whatever line he took it would not stop their exchange of anxious glances. There was no understanding, any longer, between him and them. Or rather, he still understood them, but they couldn't follow him any more.

"Will you come with me, Milleran, so that we can have a big cleaning-up?"

She followed him, bewildered, into the first office, where he did not bend down right away to the bottom shelf, but took out Volume III of *Vidal-Lablacbe*, where there was a document of disastrous import to a man who had been in past Cabinets and would doubtless be in future ones.

Still holding this, he put back the book and went on to another and yet another, plucking out now a letter, now a scrap of paper that had been crumpled, as its creases still showed.

"Why have you turned so pale, Milleran? You look as though you were going to faint."

Yet he wasn't looking at her. He simply knew. Then, turning at last to the Pierre Louÿs volume, he went on again, in an encouraging tone with no shade of blame or anger:

"You knew all this, didn't you?"

Thereupon, as he straightened up again, adding Chalamont's confession to the other papers in his hand, she burst into tears, took a few steps toward the door as though to run away into the darkness, changed her mind, came back to fling herself at his feet, and tried to grab his hand.

"Forgive me, sir . . . didn't want to, I swear I didn't. . . . "

This immediately restored his peremptory, authoritative manner, for he could never abide tears, bursts of emotion, any more than he could tolerate certain kinds of rudeness or silliness. He wouldn't have any woman writhing on the ground, kissing his hand and dropping tears on it.

He commanded her:

"Get up!"

Then, his tone already gentler:

"Steady, Milleran . . . There's nothing to be excited about. . . . "

"I assure you, sir, that . . . "

"You did as you were told to do, and quite right too. *By whom?*"

He was in a hurry for her to recover herself, to emerge

from this melodramatic atmosphere, and in order to help
her he went to the length of patting her shoulder, an unusual gesture with him.

"Who was it?"

"Superintendent Dolomieu."

"When?"

She hesitated.

"When I was still in Paris?"

"No. About two years ago. I had a day off and went to
Etretat, and he was there, waiting for me. He said it was part
of his official duty, he was giving me instructions on behalf
of the government. . . . "

"The government was quite right, and I should probably have done the same myself. You were asked to copy the
papers?"

She shook her head, and another sob jerked out. There
was still a shiny, damp track down one of her cheeks.

"No. Inspector Aillevard has a photostat machine in his
room. . . . "

"So you used to give him the papers and he returned
them next day?"

"Sometimes only an hour later. Not one is missing. I
took care he gave them all back to me."

She couldn't understand the Premier's attitude, couldn't
manage to believe in it. Instead of being angry or downcast,
as she would have expected, he showed a calm she had seldom known him to display, and his face was lit by a smile.

One would have thought he found it a good game, which
amused him more than anyone.

"As things are now, it won't matter much if we destroy
these papers, will it?"

She was trying to smile too, almost succeeding, for there

was something detached and airy about him which was infectious. This was the first time he had ever seemed to regard her as an equal, so that their relationship took on a personal touch.

"Perhaps it would be better, all the same, for the originals to be got rid of. . . . "

He showed her the Chalamont letter. "Did you find that?"

She nodded, not without a shade of pride.

Funny thing! If Chalamont has chosen an inquisitive fellow as his Minister of the Interior, and if the chap happens to send for his chief's file . . . "

He knew Dolomieu, who had been under his orders and was Director of General Information at the Rue des Saussaies. Would he take advantage of Chalamont's access to power to get himself appointed Director of the Sureté Nationale, or even Prefect of Police?

What did it matter, after all!

"Since you know where these papers are, come and help me. . . . "

In the first room she only missed two, whose places of concealment he pointed out to her with childish satisfaction.

"So you hadn't found those?"

In the second room, she had found all his hiding places; in his study she had missed only one.

If the policeman on duty was watching them through the window he must have been surprised to see the Premier and his secretary bending over the hearth, throwing in papers that burned with tall, roaring flames.

"We shall have to burn the books as well."

"What books?"

So she hadn't thought of the American edition of his

memoirs, and she was astounded to see its pages black with notes, probably wondering when he could have written them without her knowledge.

"No point in burning the bindings, they're too thick, and we mustn't put too many pages at a time into the fire."

It was a long job tearing out the pages a few at a time and stirring them with the tongs to help them burn. While she was squatting down and attending to it, he stood behind her.

"Madame Blanche as well?" he asked, knowing she would understand.

She did understand, gave an affirmative gesture, added, after a moment's reflection:

"She couldn't have done otherwise. . . . "

He hesitated to name anyone else.

"Emile?"

"From the very beginning."

In other words, Emile had already been reporting on his behavior to the Rue des Saussaies when he was still a Cabinet Minister, then Premier.

Hadn't he always known it at the back of his mind, he who had considered it his duty to have other people spied on?

Or had he been ingenuous? Cunning? Needing to feel that he was an exception, that the rules didn't apply to him?

"And Gabrielle?"

"That's not the same thing. In Paris, when you were away from home, an inspector came now and then to ask her questions. . . . "

He had been standing for too long, and he felt the need to sit down, in his place, his armchair, in his usual position. It was as comforting as getting home and slipping on one's old clothes. The tall, dancing flames were roasting him down one side and on one cheek, but it would soon be over. As his elbow knocked against the silent radio set, where it stood on the desk, unneeded from now on, he said:

"Take this too. . . . "

She misunderstood him, or pretended to misunderstand, so as to do her bit to cheer up a situation that was depressing her:

"You want to burn the radio?"

He gave a faint chuckle.

"Give it to whoever you like."

"May I keep it myself . . . ?"

She stopped herself just in time from adding:

" . . . as a souvenir."

He had understood, but he didn't scowl. He had never seemed so gentle in all his life, and he was like one of those old men who are to be seen in the country or the suburbs, sitting in sunny doorways, gazing for hours on end at a tree or some drifting clouds.

"I'm sure Gaffé will have telephoned to Dr. Lalinde."

Now he had confided in her, she was ready to reciprocate.

"Yes. He said he was going to."

"Was he very frightened when he found me asleep?"

"He didn't know you'd taken the medicine."

"What about you?"

She didn't answer, and he realized he mustn't begin to pester them with questions. They, too, had done what they could, like Xavier, like Chalamont, like that swine Dolomieu.

What did the word "swine" remind him of?

"*That swine* . . . "

He couldn't recall it, and yet when the word had been spoken it had seemed to be of considerable importance.

There was a name on the tip of his tongue, but why make the effort? Now he'd come full circle, that kind of thing had ceased to concern him.

It was a strange impression, agreeable and a little terrifying, not needing to think any longer.

A few more flames, a few pages writhing and then falling to ashes between the tongs, and all threads would be severed.

Gabrielle would come to announce that the Premier's dinner was waiting for him. The Premier would follow her obediently, would sit down on the chair offered by young Marie, with her perpetual dread of his sitting down on air. He wasn't hungry. He would eat, to please them. He would answer the questions put to him by Gaffé when he came, perhaps accompanied by Lalinde, around seven o'clock, and he'd allow his pulse to be taken yet again, let himself be put to bed as he'd promised.

He wouldn't be sarcastic with any of them, not even ironical with Lalinde, who was always a shade pompous.

He would only be unfailingly patient from now on, only taking care not to cry out, not to call for help, when the moment arrived. He meant to see to that by himself, decently, with discretion.

Whether it came tomorrow, in a week, or in a year, he would wait, and when his glance fell on Sully's memoirs, he murmured:

"You can put that book away."

What was the sense of reading other people's recollections any longer? It didn't interest him, neither did any other book, and they could have burned the whole library for all he cared.

"There we are!"

There had been nothing dramatic about it, when all was said and done, and he was almost pleased with himself. There was even a gleam of mischief in his gray eyes as he thought about his household's reactions.

Seeing him so calm and gentle, wouldn't they shake their heads sadly and whisper behind his back:

"Have you noticed how he's sinking?"

Gabrielle, no doubt, would add:

"Like a lamp dying down. . . . "

Merely because he'd ceased to concern himself with their little affairs.

"Are you asleep?" Milleran inquired anxiously, noticing all of a sudden that his eyes were closed.

He shook his head, raised his lids, smiled at her as though she were not only Milleran, but the whole of the human race.

"No, my child."

He added, after a moment's silence:

"Not yet."

Noland, October 14, 1957

THE NEVERSINK LIBRARY

AFTER MIDNIGHT
by Irmgard Keun

978-1-935554-41-7
$15.00 / $17.00 CAN

THE ETERNAL PHILISTINE
by Ödön von Horvath

978-1-935554-47-9
$15.00 / $17.00 CAN

THE LATE LORD BYRON
by Doris Langley Moore

978-1-935554-48-6
$18.95 / $21.50 CAN

THE TRAIN
by Georges Simenon

978-1-935554-46-2
$14.00 / $16.00 CAN

**THE AUTOBIOGRAPHY OF
A SUPER-TRAMP**
by W. H. Davies

978-1-61219-022-8
$15.00 / $17.00 CAN

FAITHFUL RUSLAN
by Georgi Vladimov

978-1-935554-67-7
$15.00 / $17.00 CAN

THE PRESIDENT
by Georges Simenon

978-1-935554-62-2
$14.00 / $16.00 CAN

THE WAR WITH THE NEWTS
by Karel Capek

978-1-61219-023-5
$15.00 / $17.00 CAN

AMBIGUOUS ADVENTURE
by Cheikh Hamidou Kane

978-1-61219-054-9
$15.00 / $17.00 CAN

THE DEVIL IN THE FLESH
by Raymond Radiguet

978-1-61219-056-3
$15.00 / $17.00 CAN

**THE MADONNA OF THE
SLEEPING CARS**
by Maurice Dekobra

978-1-61219-058-7
$15.00 / $17.00 CAN

THE BOOK OF KHALID
by Ameen Rihani

978-1-61219-087-7
$15.00 / $17.00 CAN

Hound of the Baskervilles

A Play in Two Acts

Adapted and Dramatized by
Tim Kelly

From the Classic Thriller of
Sir Arthur Conan Doyle

A SAMUEL FRENCH ACTING EDITION

SAMUEL
FRENCH

FOUNDED 1830

New York Hollywood London Toronto

SAMUELFRENCH.COM

CHARACTERS
(*In Order of Appearance*)

LADY AGATHA MORTIMER: A medical doctor, ample, "tweedy", forceful

PERKINS: a young maid

WATSON: Holmes' colleague

SHERLOCK HOLMES: a famed private investigator interested in bizarre cases, a master at detection

MRS. BARRYMORE: the housekeeper

SIR HENRY: a young nobleman, heir to a fortune and a curse

BARRYMORE: a butler, slightly sinister, but capable

KATHY STAPLETON: a vivacious young woman

JACK: her brother, given to emotional outbursts

LAURA LYONS: a capable young woman with a dangerous secret

STORY OF THE PLAY

The greatest of all Sherlock Holmes adventures! Adapted to a modern setting that takes literature's most spine-chilling mystery and turns it into a play of suspense, humor and ultimate terror. Sir Henry has become heir to the vast Baskerville fortune, a legacy that comes complete with a family curse—death at the fangs of a living horror prowling the English moor. Only Sherlock Holmes can stop the beast from striking again. While mysterious lights signal Baskerville Hall, and the hound terrifies the countryside, the sleuthing begins and suspicion falls on sinister servants, butterfly collectors, ladies in distress, and escaped convicts. Who wrote the letter that summoned the hound? Why do its eyes emit flame? What is the significance of the prehistoric huts dotting the moor? Is Sir Henry's romance with the lovely Kathy doomed? Is the supernatural at work? Audiences will have a terrific time attempting to discover the true killer—and reacting to the surprise twist. When the chills and shrieks settle down, there's always a laugh to relieve the rising tension. Excellent character roles, one simple set, no production problems, designed for easy rehearsals. Modern clothes for costuming. Suitable for all groups. "Opening night audience gripped the edge of its collective seat. Fun from start to finish." . . . Bibolet, ARIZONA AFTER DARK . . . " . . . will no doubt terrorize a large number of theatergoers." . . . PHOENIX GAZETTE . . . "Fun isn't so much in the ghost hound as it is in the writing. Professional, witty, suspenseful. Conan Doyle would be pleased." . . . HOLMESIAN TATTLER.

4

SYNOPSIS

PLACE: Baskerville Hall, a manor house on the moor in the west country of England.

TIME: The Present.

ACT ONE

SCENE 1: A large sitting room. Early afternoon.

SCENE 2: A few days later.

SCENE 3: Still later in the week. Night.

ACT TWO

SCENE 1: The sitting room. Two days later.

SCENE 2: That night.

SCENE 3: The following evening

The Hound of the Baskervilles

ACT ONE

SCENE 1

SETTING: *A large sitting room in Baskerville Hall, a manor house located on the English moor. It's a melancholy room with the scent of age and tradition in every corner. Stage Right there's a fireplace with a chair on each side. Above the fireplace there's a portrait of* SIR HUGO BASKERVILLE, *an 18th century aristocrat, brutal, cruel, insensitive. Upstage Center is an entry hall that leads into other parts of the house, with exits Right and Left, with a few steps in view, Left, if possible, to indicate a stairway to the upper floors. On each side of the entry, in the room, there are bookshelves or, perhaps, tables with books, statuary, candlesticks or lamps, etc. Stage Left are French doors that open out to the moor surrounding Baskerville Hall. Down Left there is a writing desk that faces the wall with a chair in front of it. Down Right Center there is a chaise lounge or a small sofa. Down Left Center there is a fine chair with a small side table on the Upstage side. Additional stage dressing will greatly enhance the stage picture; rugs, books, wall tapestries, et al; but about everything hangs a heavy aura of the past—as if the room were about to be turned into a museum. The set is also suited to drapes.*

TIME: *Present. Early afternoon.*

7

AT RISE: LADY AGATHA MORTIMER, *a rather ample woman dressed in tweeds, is seated at the desk pouring over some document. She is quite aware of the contents and reads to reacquaint herself with certain facts.*

LADY AGATHA. "Of the origin of the Hound of the Baskervilles there have been many statements, yet as I come in a direct line from Hugo Baskerville, and as I had the story from my own father, who also had it from his, I have set it down with all belief that it occurred even as is here set forth . . . "

(PERKINS, *a maid, enters Up Center, from Right.*)

PERKINS. He's still not back, Lady Agatha. No sign of him from the upstairs windows, either.

LADY AGATHA. (*Turns, worried.*) You shouldn't have allowed him to go, Perkins.

PERKINS. It's not my place to stop Sir Henry if he wants to go out.

LADY AGATHA. He doesn't know the moor as we do. You know how treacherous it can be.

PERKINS. Indeed, I do, m'am. Only yesterday another pony went under the mud at Grimpen Mire.

LADY AGATHA. A false step there is sure death.

PERKINS. Anyhow, Barrymore's gone to fetch him back.

LADY AGATHA. Good. (*Stands, moves Center.*) I'm expecting a Dr. Watson and a Mr. Holmes shortly. Show them in the minute they arrive.

PERKINS. I will, m'am. Will you be wanting tea?

LADY AGATHA. Yes. For four. Sir Henry will be joining us, I trust.

(PERKINS *exits.* DR. JOHN WATSON *enters through the open French doors, exuberant and hale.*)

WATSON. Ah, there you are, Lady Agatha. Not late, am I?

LADY AGATHA. (*She moves to him. They shake hands.*) You'll never know how thankful I am for your presence, Watson. (*Looks Left.*) Where is Mr. Holmes?

WATSON. He'll be along shortly.

LADY AGATHA. (*Indicates sofa.*) I've arranged for tea.

WATSON. (*Crosses, sits.*) I hope you won't take offense, but you do seem distraught. Not like you at all. There's one thing I always remember about you from those days we worked together at the hospital. Nerves of steel and a disposition to match.

LADY AGATHA. Thank you, Watson. I appreciate that. To tell the truth I have been on edge. Desperate, some might say.

WATSON. Desperate?

LADY AGATHA. When I heard you and Mr. Holmes were on holiday nearby, I wasted no time getting in touch.

WATSON. Not exactly a holiday. Holmes has always been fascinated by the grim charm of this locale, especially the traces of the prehistoric people who lived here.

LADY AGATHA. You mean the stone huts dotting the moors. They do give one the feeling of another time.

WATSON. Downright creepy if you ask me.

LADY AGATHA. I wouldn't be at all surprised to see a skin-clad hairy man crawl out from one of those huts.

WATSON. Doing what may I ask?

LADY AGATHA. Fitting a flint-tipped arrow on to the string of his bow.

WATSON. I'm not given much to flights of fancy. Imagination is more in Holmes' line.

LADY AGATHA. I'm looking forward to meeting him.

HOLMES. (*He enters via the French doors.*) And so you shall, Lady Agatha.

LADY AGATHA. (*They shake hands.*) A very great pleasure for me, Mr. Holmes.

HOLMES. Kind of you to say so. I trust you enjoyed your walk around the excavations at Grimpen Mire. The south section, I believe.

LADY AGATHA. How do you know I've been there?

HOLMES. You left your walking stick outside. The tip is coated with a reddish clay that is found only in that area.

LADY AGATHA. You live up to your reputation.

HOLMES. Judging from the consistency of the clay you were there within the last three hours.

LADY AGATHA. Bravo.

HOLMES. I would be cautious if you take your schnauzer there. They have a tendency to move impulsively. Miniature, I should imagine.

LADY AGATHA. How do you know I even have a dog?

HOLMES. Teeth marks on the walking stick. Obviously the dog is in the habit of carrying it from time to time. The jaw, as indicated by the space between the marks, is not large. That and— (*He plucks a bit of hair from* LADY AGATHA'S *tweeds.*) this small puff of silver-gray dog fur leads me to surmise—a miniature schnauzer.

WATSON. You really are an automaton, Holmes. A calculating machine. There is something positively inhuman about you at times.

LADY AGATHA. (*She sits Down Left Center.*) You take my breath away, Mr. Holmes.

HOLMES. Elementary.

WATSON. You said you needed our help.

LADY AGATHA. I do.

HOLMES. (*Moves Center.*) Does your request, in some way, concern itself with the recent demise of Sir Charles Baskerville?

LADY AGATHA. It does.

WATSON. London papers said it was a heart attack.

HOLMES. An elderly gentleman, if I recall correctly.

LADY AGATHA. Over eighty.

HOLMES. You suspect foul play.

LADY AGATHA. What makes you say that?

HOLMES. You would hardly have called upon my services if the situation were not grave.

LADY AGATHA. I have always considered myself a rational woman. Watson can vouch for that.

WATSON. Absolutely.

LADY AGATHA. I've never taken the occult seriously.

WATSON. The occult?

LADY AGATHA. (*She stands, Crosses to desk, picks up document.*) Perhaps this will explain. (*She steps back, hands the document to* HOLMES.)

HOLMES. (*Scans it.*) Early eighteen century, unless it's a forgery.

LADY AGATHA. It is no forgery.

WATSON. What is it?

HOLMES. I'm not unfamiliar with the contents. (*To* WATSON.) It purports to describe the origin of the curse of the Baskervilles.

WATSON. Curse?

HOLMES. Come, come, Watson. Common knowledge.

WATSON. May be common knowledge to you, but not to me.

(LADY AGATHA *Crosses to fireplace, studies the portrait of Sir Hugo.*)

HOLMES. (*Studying the document.*) The exact date is 1742. (*Recalls the legend.*) Sir Hugo Baskerville was a villain, a coarse man given to excesses of intemperance and rage. He came to love, if that word can be used with his sort, a village girl. He kidnapped her, kept her prisoner in this house, while night after night he and his foul companions revelled below, probably in this very room.

(WATSON *looks around as if he expected Sir Hugo to materialize.*)

LADY AGATHA. (*Looking at portrait.*) He has much to answer for.

HOLMES. One night, with the aid cf the stout ivy outside her window, she made her escape.

WATSON. Good for her.

HOLMES. There's more to it than that, Watson. Sir Hugo gave chase over the moor. His companions-in-drink riding at his heels. He outdistanced them. (*Checks the document again.*) Sir Hugo's companions found him on the moor. By the two great stones.

LADY AGATHA. You can see them from the windows. They marked the door to some long-forgotten temple.

WATSON. I have seen them, frightening things ir the moonlight.

HOLMES. When they came on the spot, the village girl had expired. Fallen dead of fear and fatigue.

WATSON. And Sir Hugo?

HOLMES. He was by her side. Also dead. But that wasn't what terrified the friends that found him.

WATSON. What did?

HOLMES. (*He hands him the document; indicates a passage.*) Read it for yourself.

WATSON. " . . . and plucking at his throat, there stood a foul thing, a great black beast, shaped like a hound, yet larger than any hound that ever mortal eye has rested upon. And even as they looked the thing tore the throat out of Hugo Baskerville."

LADY AGATHA. Many of the family have been unhappy in their deaths. Sudden, bloody, mysterious.

WATSON. Surely you don't believe this mumbo-jumbo?

HOLMES. (*Takes back the document.*) It is obvious the Baskerville who wrote the account did. (*Reads.*) "I counsel you by way of caution to forbear frcm crossing the moor in those dark hours when the powers of evil are exalted."

WATSON. (*Scoffs.*) Powers of evil, ir.deed. It's a fairy tale.

LADY AGATHA. Sir Charles believed in the curse.

HOLMES. As I recall, Sir Charles was only in residence for a few years.

LADY AGATHA. That is correct. His business interests, mainly those in South Africa, kept him away.

HOLMES. Who looked after Baskerville Hall?

LADY AGATHA. The Barrymores. A married couple. He acts as butler, she as housekeeper.

HOLMES. Still in service here?

LADY AGATHA. Oh, yes. It was Barrymore who found the body. It was Sir Charles' habit each night to take a walk before retiring.

HOLMES. But never onto the moor.

LADY AGATHA. Never.

WATSON. Because of that silly legend?

HOLMES. Watson, please. Do continue, Lady Agatha.

LADY AGATHA. The night of his death he went out as usual. He never returned.

HOLMES. No sign of violence on the body?

LADY AGATHA. None.

WATSON. At his advanced age he probably passed on from cardiac exhaustion.

LADY AGATHA. Exactly.

HOLMES. Who performed the police autopsy?

LADY AGATHA. I did.

HOLMES. The coroner's jury accepted the medical evidence?

LADY AGATHA. There was no reason not to.

HOLMES. Lady Agatha, it is not what you're saying that I find of interest, rather what you're not saying.

LADY AGATHA. If you weren't a private investigator, Mr. Holmes, I would suspect you of being a psychic.

HOLMES. (*He goes to the desk, sets down the document.* LADY AGATHA *moves Center.*) Why not come directly to the point?

LADY AGATHA. I believe Sir Charles was . . . "frightened to death."

HOLMES. Proof?

LADY AGATHA. Within the last few months it became increasingly plain to me that Sir Charles' nervous system was strained to the breaking point.

HOLMES. I asked for proof. *Facts.*

LADY AGATHA. The expression on his face was one of sheer terror.

WATSON. Easily explained by a muscle spasm.

LADY AGATHA. There was one false statement made by Barrymore at the inquest.

HOLMES. Oh?

LADY AGATHA. He said there were no tracks on the ground round the body.

HOLMES. You said a "false" statement.

LADY AGATHA. Perhaps Barrymore didn't see what I saw.

WATSON. Which was?

LADY AGATHA. My motive for witholding it from the coroner's inquiry is that a person of science shrinks from placing one's self in a position of seeming to endorse a popular superstition.

HOLMES. In other words you did see footprints.

LADY AGATHA. Yes. A distance off, but fresh and clear.

WATSON. Why conceal the fact?

LADY AGATHA. I have already explained my reason.

HOLMES. The footprints. A man's or a woman's?

LADY AGATHA. (*She pauses. Her voice drops low.*) They were the footprints of a gigantic hound.

(WATSON and HOLMES *exchange a guarded look.* MRS. BARRYMORE, *a severe sort of woman Enters Up Center from Left.*)

MRS. BARRYMORE. Beg pardon, Lady Agatha. It's Sir Henry. I saw him from upstairs. He's cutting across the moor now.

LADY AGATHA. Thank heaven.

HOLMES. You're the housekeeper, I take it.

MRS. BARRYMORE. Yes, sir. Mrs. Barrymore.

HOLMES. How long have you been in service at Baskerville Hall?

(MRS. BARRYMORE *looks to* LADY AGATHA, *bewildered by the questions.*)

LADY AGATHA. It's quite all right, Mrs. Barrymore. This is Mr. Sherlock Holmes.

MRS. BARRYMORE. I've been in service here most of my life.

HOLMES. Then you know the moor.

MRS. BARRYMORE. I grew up on the moor, Mr. Holmes.

LADY AGATHA. Mrs. Barrymore and her husband know more about Baskerville Hall than anyone in the county.

MRS. BARRYMORE. If you have no other questions, sir. I'll see to my duties.

HOLMES. I have no other questions at this time. (MRS. BARRYMORE *nods and Exits Up Center, turns Right.*) Remarkable woman. Reminds me of Aimee Small, the noted axe murderess of Charing Cross.

SIR HENRY. (*He Enters via the French doors. A good-looking young man.*) Ah, I see you've finally caught him in your net, Lady Agatha.

LADY AGATHA. Henry, you mustn't wander over the countryside until you know more of the place.

SIR HENRY. Nonsense. I stuck to the paths and the light was excellent. I was visiting with Kathy.

LADY AGATHA. (*She moves behind the sofa.*) I sent Barrymore to go and look for you.

SIR HENRY. (*Moves Center, extends his hand to Watson.*) It's a pleasure for me, Mr. Holmes.

WATSON. (*Stands, shakes.*) Thank you, but I'm not Holmes. I'm John Watson, M.D., a former colleague of Lady Agatha's. (*He nods to* HOLMES *at desk.*)

SIR HENRY. You'll forgive me. (*He moves Down Center.* HOLMES *meets him halfway. They shake.*)

HOLMES. I take it from the timbre of your accent that you've spent some time in America, Sir Henry.

SIR HENRY. The States and Canada. I only recently returned. If it hadn't been for my uncle's death, I'd still be there.

WATSON. Surely you don't believe the balderdash Lady Agatha has been spouting. (*Turns to* LADY AGATHA, *apologetic.*) I beg your pardon, my dear.

HOLMES. Watson has never been noted for an abundance of tact. (WATSON *pouts, sits on the sofa.*) Do you share Lady Agatha's doubts about your uncle's death?

SIR HENRY. I haven't made up my mind.

LADY AGATHA. Show him the letter.

HOLMES. Letter?

SIR HENRY. (*He sits Down Left Center takes out a wallet and from it plucks a folded piece of stationery.*) This arrived one morning at my London hotel. (*He hands it to* HOLMES *who unfolds it.*)

HOLMES. Words cut from the *London Times* and gummed to the paper.

WATSON. Rather an old-fashioned gambit, eh, Holmes?

HOLMES. Arsenic is old-fashioned too, Watson, but it does the trick.

LADY AGATHA. How can you tell it's *The Times?*

HOLMES. *Times* print is entirely distinctive. These words could have been taken from nothing else. (*Reads aloud.*) "As you value your life or your reason keep away from the moor."

WATSON. (*To* LADY AGATHA.) Nothing supernatural about that.

HOLMES. It might have been sent by someone who was convinced that Sir Charles' death was . . . "unearthly."

WATSON. Who?

HOLMES. Someone trying to frighten Sir Henry from Baskerville Hall. No envelope, no stamp?

SIR HENRY. I found it tucked under the door of my room.

HOLMES. You intend to remain in residence here, Sir Henry?

SIR HENRY. There is no man on earth, or devil in hell who can prevent me from staying in my own home.

HOLMES. I take that as a final answer?

SIR HENRY. Absolutely.

HOLMES. Then you did well to seek me out, Lady Agatha. May I keep this? (*The letter.*)

SIR HENRY. Of course.

HOLMES. (*To* LADY AGATHA.) Anything found near the body?

LADY AGATHA. The stub of Sir Charles' cigar. Two stubs actually, and a great deal of cigar ash.

HOLMES. (*Ponders this.*) Curious. (*Quick.*) There is no other claimant on the estate, I presume?

LADY AGATHA. There were three brothers. Sir Charles was the elder. The second died young.

SIR HENRY. That was my father.

HOLMES. And the third?

LADY AGATHA. Rodger Baskerville. A black sheep. Fled to Central America and died there of tropical fever.

HOLMES. Supposing that anything happened to our young friend here—you'll forgive the unpleasant hypothesis—who would then inherit?

LADY AGATHA. Since Rodger died unmarried, the estate would descend to James Desmond.

SIR HENRY. A distant cousin.

WATSON. Is there any other kind? (*He chuckles.*)

HOLMES. Watson, please. (WATSON *pouts.*)

SIR HENRY. He's a clergyman in the village of Tracey Coombes.

HOLMES. Quite close, actually.

SIR HENRY. It's a short drive.

HOLMES. Who profited by Sir Charles' will?

LADY AGATHA. There were many insignificant sums to individuals and a large number of charities.

SIR HENRY. He was a generous man.

HOLMES. (*Impatient.*) Yes, yes.

SIR HENRY. The Barrymores each received five thousand pounds.

WATSON. (*Impressed.*) He *was* generous.

HOLMES. Did they know they would receive this sum?

LADY AGATHA. Sir Charles was fond of talking about the provisions of his will.

HOLMES. Unwise.

LADY AGATHA. I hope you won't suspect everyone who profited. After all, Sir Charles left me ten thousand.

WATSON. (*He gives a long, low whistle.* HOLMES *freezes him with a stare. He swallows hard.*) Sorry.

LADY AGATHA. You will take the case, Mr. Holmes?

HOLMES. (*Lost in thought.*) Hmmmmm?

LADY AGATHA. You will take the case.

HOLMES. (*Brisk.*) Out of the question.

LADY AGATHA. But you must.

SIR HENRY. We've been counting on you, Mr. Holmes.

HOLMES. I'm due in Bristol sometime tomorrow, then I must spend a few days in London.

SIR HENRY. If it's a question of money—

HOLMES. My professional charges are on a fixed scale. I do not vary them, except when I remit them altogether.

WATSON. Holmes, surely you can let other matters wait.

HOLMES. You know my methods. (*To* LADY AGATHA *and* SIR HENRY.) I will do my best to settle my prior obligations as quickly as possible. In the meantime, I shall leave Watson here to look out for you, Sir Henry.

SIR HENRY. Whatever you think best.

HOLMES. Please follow his advice. I trust him implicitly. (*To* WATSON.) You will communicate anything of interest to me in London.

WATSON. (*He is delighted with the "assignment."*) You can depend on it.

HOLMES. On one point I must demand complete fidelity.

SIR HENRY. What is it?

HOLMES. Under no circumstances must you venture onto the moor at night. I can't impress the importance of this enough.

LADY AGATHA. Then you do believe the legend?

HOLMES. You understand, Watson?

WATSON. I do.

HOLMES. (*Moves for open doors.*) There's something in the air that disturbs me.

SIR HENRY. The air? What's in the air, Mr. Holmes?

HOLMES. (*Turns back.*) The scent of murder, Sir Henry. *Murder.* (HOLMES *Exits. The others look after him and, then, nervously to each other.*)

CURTAIN

ACT ONE

SCENE 2

AT RISE: *A few days later.* WATSON *is seated Down Left Center checking a large map.* BARRYMORE, *a dour-looking man, Enters Upstage Center.*

BARRYMORE. You wanted to see me, Dr. Watson?

WATSON. (*Turns.*) Ah, Barrymore. Yes. I don't know quite how to put this.

BARRYMORE. (*Doesn't understand.*) Sir?

WATSON. I mean, I'm not altogether sure of what I heard. (BARRYMORE *looks puzzled.*) Last night, close to midnight, did you hear the sound of a woman sobbing?

BARRYMORE. I did not.

WATSON. Hmmmm.

BARRYMORE. Perhaps it was the wind. The wind racing on the moor can make all sorts of strange noises.

WATSON. The sound was most certainly in the house, not on the moor. I thought, perhaps, it might have been Mrs. Barrymore.

BARRYMORE. We share the same room, Doctor. If my wife were crying I would have known.

WATSON. Could it have been Perkins?

BARRYMORE. Highly unlikely. Perkins seldom spends the night. She lives with her family on the Grimpen Mire road.

WATSON. (*He is certain of what he heard, but realizes he isn't going to get anywhere with* BARRYMORE.) You may be right. The wind racing on the moor.

BARRYMORE. I'll be going into the village later this afternoon, Doctor Watson. Is there anything I might get for you?

WATSON. No, thank you, Barrymore. I'll be going in myself.

BARRYMORE. Very good, sir. (*Turns to Exit.*)

WATSON. One moment, Barrymore.

BARRYMORE. (*Faces* WATSON.) Sir?

WATSON. You've been in service here for quite some time.

BARRYMORE. My father was the caretaker. My family has looked after the Hall for four generations.

WATSON. In that case, you know the families that inhabit the moor.

BARRYMORE. I do.

WATSON. (*Back to the map.*) I see the cottage that belongs to Lady Agatha, and Baskerville Hall clearly marked, but who lives here . . . (*Indicates.*) northeast of the great rocks?

BARRYMORE. That would be the house of Mr. Frankland.

WATSON. (*Recalls the name.*) Frankland? An elderly man, choleric, with a beard.

BARRYMORE. You've met him then, Doctor Watson?

WATSON. Bumped into at the post office. Disagreeable sort.

BARRYMORE. (*Steps Downstage.*) His passion is for the British law.

WATSON. Sues people, they tell me.

BARRYMORE. He's spent a considerable fortune in litigation. Mr. Frankland fights for the mere pleasure of fighting. He's ready to take up either side of a question as long as he can have his day in court.

WATSON. I know the sort. (*Indicates.*) And this cottage?

BARRYMORE. Mr. Stapleton and his sister.

WATSON. Ah, Sir Henry's friend. What's she like?

BARRYMORE. Quite lively.

WATSON. And her brother?

BARRYMORE. I've only met him on one occasion. On the moor. Chasing butterflies.

WATSON. Butterflies?

BARRYMORE. (*Confirms.*) Butterflies.

WATSON. (*Clarifying.*) So what we have close by are the homes of the Stapletons, Lady Agatha and Mr. Frankland.

BARRYMORE. There are other cottages on the moor, but they're in bad repair, quite unlivable.

WATSON. If you don't mind me saying so, Barrymore, things are a bit backward in this region.

BARRYMORE. Sir Charles was doing his best to remedy the situation, that's why his death was such a loss.

WATSON. Mr. Frankland lives alone?

BARRYMORE. He does now.

WATSON. No family?

BARRYMORE. He has a daughter.

WATSON. Where is she? (*Laughter from outside.*)

BARRYMORE. (*Moves Up Center, looks out the open French doors.*) That would be Sir Henry.

WATSON. What about Mr. Frankland's daughter?

BARRYMORE. (*Still looking off.*) Miss Stapleton is with him.

WATSON. Never mind about Miss Stapleton. I asked you about Mr. Frankland's daughter.

BARRYMORE. (*Anxious to avoid the topic.*) Her name was Laura.

WATSON. Why are you making such a mystery out of it?

SIR HENRY. (*He Enters, calling over his shoulder.*) Never mind the flowers. I want a bit of lunch.

WATSON. You look as if you've been enjoying yourself.

SIR HENRY. Kathy took me on a tour of the old huts. The moor is riddled with old mine shafts, too. I didn't know that. (BARRYMORE *clears his throat.*) What is it, Barrymore?

BARRYMORE. I wonder if I might have a word with you, Sir Henry.

SIR HENRY. Certainly, what is it? (BARRYMORE *looks to* WATSON, *meaning he wants to speak in private.*)

WATSON. (*Stands.*) I'll go and introduce myself to your young friend.

SIR HENRY. We won't be long. (WATSON *Exits via French doors.* SIR HENRY *moves Down Left.*) Well?

BARRYMORE. My wife and I will be happy, Sir Henry, to stay with you until you have made fresh arrangements.

SIR HENRY. What is that supposed to mean?

BARRYMORE. Under the new conditions this house will require considerable staff.

SIR HENRY. I wish I understood what you're driving at. What "new conditions"?

BARRYMORE. I only meant that Sir Charles led a retired life and we were able to look after his wants.

You would, naturally, wish to have more company, and so you will need changes in your household.

SIR HENRY. I'm quite comfortable with you and your wife. Isn't Perkins of some help?

BARRYMORE. She's a village girl, sir. Not terribly bright. Not accustomed to service. So few are these days.

SIR HENRY. What you're really saying is that you and your wife wish to leave.

BARRYMORE. Only when it is convenient for you, sir.

SIR HENRY. This is bad news. I'm sorry to begin my life here by breaking an old family connection.

BARRYMORE. My wife and I were both attached to Sir Charles. His death gave us a shock.

SIR HENRY. It didn't exactly give me a sense of security, Barrymore.

BARRYMORE. No, sir. But we fear we'll never again be easy in our minds at Baskerville Hall.

SIR HENRY. What do you intend to do?

BARRYMORE. We shall establish ourselves in some business. Sir Charles' generosity has given us the means to do so.

SIR HENRY. I won't try to stop you. We'll talk about this later.

BARRYMORE. Yes, sir. (BARRYMORE *Exits Upstage Center.* SIR HENRY *is unhappy.*)

KATHY. (*She sticks her head in from the outside.*) Is it safe?

SIR HENRY. Barrymore's left, if that's what you mean.

KATHY. (*Calls over her shoulder.*) Come along, Doctor. The coast is clear. (*She sweeps In. She is an attractive young woman, vital, alert and altogether captivating. She carries flowers.*) We ought to put these in water.

SIR HENRY. I'll ring for Perkins. (*He moves to some bell rope on the wall.* KATHY *moves to the sofa, sits.* WATSON *Enters.*)

KATHY. (*The flowers.*) They don't last long. It's a pity.

SIR HENRY. Yes, it is. The moor needs color.

KATHY. (*Holds up the bouquet.*) Aren't they lovely, Doctor?

WATSON. (*He moves to the sofa. The sly rogue.*) They are when you hold them, my dear.

KATHY. Did you hear that, Henry? The Doctor knows how to dispense compliments as well as pills.

WATSON. What was all the mystery with Barrymore?

SIR HENRY. (*Steps Center.*) The Barrymores want to leave.

WATSON. What?

SIR HENRY. That's what he tells me.

KATHY. I thought the Barrymores came with the wallpaper. (WATSON *laughs.*)

SIR HENRY. So did I.

KATHY. That will present a problem. Villagers don't like to work on the moor.

WATSON. One can hardly blame them. I'm grateful Baskerville Hall has modern plumbing, but I'd feel more at home if it had a telephone.

KATHY. There are no phones on the moor. Only the village.

WATSON. That sense of isolation doesn't trouble you?

SIR HENRY. Nothing troubles Kathy. (*He sits beside her.*)

KATHY. That's not true. Especially when the mist is thick. It frightens me. (SIR HENRY *takes her hand. They smile.*)

WATSON. (*He moves Center.*) The moor is a rather odd place to find such a lovely creature.

SIR HENRY. I quite agree.

WATSON. (*Half-flirting.*) I can't help but wonder why such a vital young woman wants to tuck herself away in this corner of England.

KATHY. It wasn't exactly by choice. My brother and I had a school in the north country. I'm afraid the fates were against us.

WATSON. How so?

KATHY. A serious epidemic broke out in the school. Two of the lads never recovered.

WATSON. Bad luck, indeed.

KATHY. (SIR HENRY *pats her hand protectively.*) Our capital was used up and poor Jack was devastated. He hasn't recovered yet. Still, the moor is perfect for him.

WATSON. Why?

KATHY. He has an avid interest in botany and zoology. He keeps his mind occupied and expenses are minimal. We have books, we have our studies, and we have— (*Smiles at* SIR HENRY.) interesting neighbors. (PERKINS *Enters Up Center from Right.*)

SIR HENRY. (*Takes flowers from* KATHY.) Put this in water, will you, Perkins.

PERKINS. (*Steps down.*) Yes, sir.

KATHY. No, just bring a vase. I'll arrange them myself.

PERKINS. Yes, miss. (*She steps to* WATSON, *loud whisper.*) It's been seen again, Doctor.

WATSON. What?

PERKINS. The hound.

WATSON. (*Doesn't wish to question her with* KATHY *and* SIR HENRY *listening.*) We'll talk later, Perkins. Go along.

PERKINS. Yes, sir.

SIR HENRY. (*Stands.*) Wait.

WATSON. Let me deal with this, Sir Henry.

SIR HENRY. There's no sense in trying to protect my sensibilities, Doctor. What did you mean "The Hound"?

PERKINS. It's only that Doctor Watson asked me to report anything I heard in the village.

SIR HENRY. What did you hear?

PERKINS. It's not what I heard, Sir Henry. It's what Mr. Blake saw and heard.

SIR HENRY. Blake?

KATHY. The greengrocer. The man's a dolt.

WATSON. Well, well, what did he see and hear?

PERKINS. He was on his bicycle and he heard a long, low moan sweep over the moor.

KATHY. I've heard it once or twice myself.

SIR HENRY. WHAT!

KATHY. (*Grins.*) The bogs make odd noises. It's the mud settling or the water rising, or something.

PERKINS. That's not what Mr. Blake said.

KATHY. My own guess would be a bittern booming.

WATSON. Good gracious. What's that?

KATHY. A very rare bird, practically extinct in England now, but all things are possible on the moor. I wouldn't be at all surprised that what Mr. Blake heard is the cry of the last of the bitterns.

SIR HENRY. That'll be all, Perkins.

PERKINS. (*Pouts that they don't believe her.*) Yes, Sir Henry. (*She Exits Up Center, turns Right.*)

SIR HENRY. Seems all the servants are in something of a mood.

WATSON. I was trying to get Barrymore to tell me about old Frankland's daughter. He pointedly avoided the subject.

SIR HENRY. He's not one for gossip.

KATHY. It's a rather sad situation. She married an artist named Lyons, who came sketching on the moor. He proved to be a blackguard and deserted her. Her father refused to have anything to do with her, because she married without his consent.

WATSON. I wonder why Barrymore couldn't have told me as much.

KATHY. When you've been here a while, you'll realize these people are clannish and protective of one another.

WATSON. If you'll excuse me, I want to have a word or two with Mrs. Barrymore. (*He Exits Up Center, turns Left.*)

SIR HENRY. I seem to have come into an inheritance with a vengeance.

KATHY. I wouldn't pay attention to village chatter. They're a superstitious lot.

SIR HENRY. The hound is the pet story of my family.

KATHY. That's a bad joke, Henry.

SIR HENRY. I've heard of the beast ever since I was in the nursery. I never thought of taking it seriously.

KATHY. You're not thinking of doing so now?

SIR HENRY. This business with my uncle confuses me. The whole thing seems boiling up in my head, and I can't get it clear yet.

KATHY. There's a sane, rational explanation for everything that's happened. (*She reaches into some pocket and produces something wrapped in tissue paper. She holds it out proudly.*) Here. For you. (*He takes the paper, unwraps, and displays a handsome pocket watch.*) I couldn't resist it.

SIR HENRY. It's a beauty.

KATHY. I saw the watch in the jeweler's window. The letter "B" is engraved on the back.

SIR HENRY. You're too generous. You won't save money giving gifts to me.

KATHY. This gift is "special".

SIR HENRY. Then I must secure something "extra" special for you. I thought I'd find no one on this desolate moor but rustics and eccentrics. (*He pulls her to her feet.*)

KATHY. I'm on the moor.

SIR HENRY. You're no eccentric, and far from being a rustic. (*He kisses her as . . . JACK STAPLETON, KATHY's brother, Enters via the French door. He's a nervous young man, given to emotional outbursts. He carries a butterfly net.*)

JACK. (*Furious.*) I'll thank you to keep your attentions from my sister, Sir Henry!

KATHY. (*Steps away from SIR HENRY.*) Jack, what's the matter with you?!

JACK. I'll deal with you later.

KATHY. Stop it!

SIR HENRY. You're behaving badly aren't you, Stapleton?

JACK. How I'm behaving is my own concern.

KATHY. (*Distressed.*) What's the matter with you?

JACK. Just because you're rich and have a title you think you can do as you want.

KATHY. (*Close to tears.*) I'm not going to stay and listen to you.

JACK. Rich and powerful—you're all the same.

(KATHY, *in tears, runs onto the moor.*)

SIR HENRY. Kathy!

JACK. (*A step in closer.*) You stay away from her. She's not for you.

SIR HENRY. It's no concern of yours. I shall see her as often as she permits it.

(WATSON *returns, stands Up Center, listening.*)

JACK. Then I'll see that she doesn't permit it.

SIR HENRY. Who do you think you are?

JACK. I won't warn you again. Stay away from Kathy. (*He turns, Exits.* SIR HENRY *moves to the French door.*)

SIR HENRY. And I'll thank you to stay away from Baskerville Hall!

WATSON. What was all that?

SIR HENRY. Stapleton. The man's a lunatic. Came in here in a rage when he saw Kathy and me together. My feelings towards his sister are nothing for me to be ashamed of. He drove her away in tears. Why should he object to me?

WATSON. Perhaps he's on the verge of some sort of breakdown. Remember, he hasn't been well.

SIR HENRY. (*Moves Stage Left.*) He's liable to do Kathy some harm.

WATSON. Be careful.

SIR HENRY. I'm not afraid of Stapleton and his bad temper.

(SIR HENRY *follows after the pair.* WATSON *steps into the room, moves to the French doors, looks off as* PERKINS *returns, a vase in her hand.*)

PERKINS. Here's the vase and water, Miss. (*She looks around.*) Where's Miss Kathy, Doctor Watson?

WATSON. Gone.

PERKINS. What about the flowers?

WATSON. (*Turns.*) On the sofa there.

PERKINS. (*She sees them, Crosses to the sofa, picks them up and Crosses to the mantle, arranges them, talking as she goes.*) I wasn't allowed to finish, sir.

WATSON. Hmmmm?

PERKINS. About Mr. Blake. He didn't only *hear* the hound.

WATSON. Oh?

PERKINS. He saw it.

WATSON. (*He moves Center.*) When?

PERKINS. Last night, sir.

WATSON. How did he describe it?

PERKINS. More like a great dark shape than anything else, moving so fast Mr. Blake feared for his own life.

WATSON. If it were only a great dark shape how could he be sure of what he saw?

PERKINS. Because it's eyes were fiery red and it was breathing flame. (*Guarded.*) Do you believe him, Doctor Watson?

WATSON. (*Pause, then:*) Yes, Perkins, I'm sorry to say I do.

PERKINS. (*She is surprised.*) Why, sir?

WATSON. Because I, myself, got a glimpse of what he saw. Last night—on the moor.

PERKINS. (*Wide-eyed.*) The hound of the Basker-villes?

WATSON. No, Perkins—a hound of hell.

CURTAIN

ACT ONE

SCENE 3

AT RISE: *Later in the week. Night. Sound of Wind Howling on the moor. Stage remains empty for a few moments.* BARRYMORE, *cautious, Enters Up Center. He looks around as if he half-expected someone to pop up any second. He looks to the portrait, speaks with a hint of sarcasm.*

BARRYMORE. Good evening to you, Sir Hugo. (*He suppresses a chuckle, Dims the Lights, so the room is in shadows. He moves to the French doors, with a flashlight in hand. He points it onto the moor, snaps it on . . . and off . . . and on . . . and off . . .*)

SIR HENRY'S VOICE. Doctor Watson, are you back?

(*Nervous,* BARRYMORE *moves Down to the desk and quickly puts the flashlight into some drawer.*)

SIR HENRY. (*He Enters Up Center from Right.*) What's happened to the lights?

BARRYMORE. I'll put them on at once, Sir Henry. (*He does so, efficient, the perfect butler.*)

SIR HENRY. So, it's you, Barrymore.

BARRYMORE. Yes, sir.

SIR HENRY. What were you doing in here in the dark?

BARRYMORE. The dark, Sir Henry?

SIR HENRY. You have an annoying habit of repeating things.

BARRYMORE. Actually, sir . . . well, the truth is . . . uh, —I'm afraid I fell asleep. (*Indicates Down Left Center chair.*)

SIR HENRY. That's most unlike you.

BARRYMORE. I suffer from headaches, sir. I felt a bit faint. I thought if I rested for a moment I'd feel better. When I awoke the dark had settled in.

SIR HENRY. (*He, again, isn't buying the explanation, but decides not to press the matter for the time being.*) If you say so. I was looking for the *Weekly Journal.*

BARRYMORE. My wife has it, sir. It came with yesterday's post.

SIR HENRY. I would like to see it.

BARRYMORE. At once, Sir Henry. (*He Exits Up Center, turns Right.*)

(SIR HENRY *takes the pocket watch from his jacket, looks at it fondly. He moves to sofa, sits holding the watch to his ear. It's not working. He frowns, begins to wind it. While this is going on, the Wind Rises and a Face Appears at the French doors. An evil face with a bristling beard. Suddenly, SIR HENRY stiffens, aware that he is not alone. The "face" outside the room puts a hand to the door, opens it . . . quietly. A Man steps into the room, staring at the heir. His clothes are ragged and his hair is matted. He looks wild and, quite possibly mad.*)

SIR HENRY. (*Without turning, wary.*) Who . . . who's there . . . ? (*Like a frightened animal, the Man darts back outside. SIR HENRY jumps to his feet, turns. He sees there is no one, but his instincts tell him otherwise.*) Who is it? (*Silence. He moves Stage Left. Wind Up. He notices the opened door.*) Watson, that you out there?

PERKINS. (*She, fast, Enters Up Center, from Right,*

with a tray hosting a mug and pitcher. Cheery.)
Here's your *Weekly Journal*, Sir Henry.

SIR HENRY. (*Startled.*) WHAT!

PERKINS. (*Gives a startled gasp.*) Sir Henry, there's
no need to jump at me.

SIR HENRY. (*Another look through the panes.*) Oh,
it's you, Perkins. I didn't mean to bark.

PERKINS. I thought you might like some warm milk,
so I've brought a pitcher and a mug. (*She moves to
the mantle or some table Right, and puts the tray
down.*)

SIR HENRY. (*Closes door.*) That was thoughtful.
How is it you're still here?

PERKINS. The mist rolled in too fast for me. I never
cross the moor on nights like this. I sleep in the small
room at the far end of the west wing.

SIR HENRY. Have you done that recently?

PERKINS. (*Doesn't understand.*) Sir?

SIR HENRY. (*Moves Center.*) Have you stayed over
in the last few weeks?

PERKINS. Once.

SIR HENRY. I wonder, Perkins, did you hear anyone—crying?

PERKINS. Crying? I don't think so. I'm a sound
sleeper. Of course, at that end of the house one might
as well be in a tomb. The walls are that thick.

SIR HENRY. (*Rubs his arms as if he were cold.*)
Tomb is exactly what this place feels like at times.

PERKINS. Would you like me to light the fire?

SIR HENRY. I'll take care of it.

PERKINS. Very good, Sir Henry.

WATSON. (*He Enters Up Center, from Right.*) It's
a miserable night out.

SIR HENRY. Did you walk back from the village?

WATSON. I did.

PERKINS. I hope you carried a torch, Doctor Watson.

WATSON. Certainly not. I have excellent night sight.
Comes from eating carrots. You should try it, Perkins.

PERKINS. Can't abide carrots, Doctor Watson. I don't like the sound of the crunch. (*She Exits Up Center.*)

WATSON. (*Moves Down Center.*) These villagers are everything Kathy Stapleton said they were. Imagine. Not liking the sound of a carrot's crunch. Silly creature. (*He sits on the sofa.*)

SIR HENRY. What news from Holmes?

WATSON. It's positively infuriating.

SIR HENRY. How so?

WATSON. Everytime I call London I get his answering machine.

SIR HENRY. Surely, he's back in London by now.

WATSON. Let's hope so. If I don't get him tomorrow, or hear from him, I think a brief holiday would do us both some good.

SIR HENRY. You mean a trip to London.

WATSON. You'll have to go with me. I couldn't leave you here alone.

SIR HENRY. I appreciate everything you're doing, but I'm not ready for a London outing. Whatever it is that's terrifying Baskerville Hall, I intend to stick it out.

WATSON. In that case, I'll remain here also.

SIR HENRY. Did you see anyone outside the house?

WATSON. When?

SIR HENRY. On your way back. (*He Crosses to the pitcher, pours himself a mug.*)

WATSON. Can't see a thing. The mist from the moors is thicker than guilt. Can't imagine why Lady Agatha favors the place.

SIR HENRY. Bit like Kathy and her brother. She lost almost everything in bad investments a few years back.

WATSON. I didn't know that. Yet, she's the sort that belongs out of the big city. I never felt she was comfortable with the rush.

SIR HENRY. (*Holds up the mug.*) Warm milk. Don't suppose you'd care for a mug?

WATSON. Milk? No, no. Why did you ask what you did? If I had seen anyone outside the house?

SIR HENRY. I heard something at the French doors. They were opened.

WATSON. (*He moves quickly to the doors, checks them.*) They're closed now.

SIR HENRY. I closed them.

WATSON. Was there anyone else in the room?

SIR HENRY. Barrymore was in here just before I came downstairs. In the dark. Said he fell asleep.

WATSON. He's an odd one.

SIR HENRY. I'm inclined to agree with you. I don't know what he was doing in this room, but I certainly don't believe he was sleeping.

WATSON. He's evasive with my questions, yet the Barrymore's and Lady Agatha were the only witnesses the night your poor uncle met his death. It's clear to me that so long as there are none of the family at Baskerville Hall, Barrymore has a mighty fine home and nothing to do. (WATSON *is aware that someone is standing out of sight in the entry hall, Left. He signals* SIR HENRY *to be quiet.*) No need to eavesdrop in the shadows, Barrymore. Come out where we can see you.

(*Long pause.* SIR HENRY *and* WATSON *turn Up Center—*MRS. BARRYMORE *comes into view.*)

SIR HENRY. Mrs. Barrymore, do you make a habit of listening in on other people's conversation?

MRS. BARRYMORE. No, Sir Henry, I do not.

WATSON. Would you care to explain your extraordinary behavior?

MRS. BARRYMORE. You're thinking ill of my husband.

WATSON. What if we are?

MRS. BARRYMORE. He's a loyal retainer. As I am. He would never do anything to harm you in anyway, Sir Henry.

WATSON. There's cold comfort in that. (MRS. BARRYMORE *takes a charred piece of stationery from some pocket.*) What have you there?

MRS. BARRYMORE. I should have spoken out before, but it was long after the inquest that I found it. I've never breathed a word about it to anyone. Not even to my husband. (*Weak.*) I wonder—may I sit down. I'm not feeling at my best.

SIR HENRY. Certainly.

MRS. BARRYMORE. (*She moves Down Left Center, sits. She hands the paper to* WATSON.) I know why Sir Charles was on the moor.

SIR HENRY. Well?

MRS. BARRYMORE. He was to meet a woman.

SIR HENRY. I don't believe it.

MRS. BARRYMORE. The letter came the morning of your uncle's death. From the village of Tracey Coombes.

WATSON. How long have you known this paper existed?

MRS. BARRYMORE. Only a few weeks ago I was cleaning out Sir Charles' study. It hadn't been touched since his death. I found the ashes of a burned letter in the back of the grate. Most of it was charred to pieces, but one little slip, the end of the page, hung together. (*She points to the paper in* WATSON's *hand.*)

WATSON. (*Reads.*) "Please, please, as you are a gentleman, burn this letter, and be by the gate on the moor at ten o'clock."

SIR HENRY. How can you be sure this is the same letter that arrived that morning?

MRS. BARRYMORE. There was a silver trim on the border of the envelope. The same trim is on the bottom of the notepaper Doctor Watson holds.

SIR HENRY. What's the woman's name?

WATSON. No name.

MRS. BARRYMORE. Only the initials. "L.L."

SIR HENRY. I can't understand why you would want to conceal this information.

MRS. BARRYMORE. Well, sir, we were both of us devoted to Sir Charles, as well might be considering all that he'd done for us. To rake this up couldn't help our poor master, and it's well to go carefully when there's a lady in the case.

WATSON. In other words you thought this communication would somehow compromise Sir Charles' reputation?

MRS. BARRYMORE. (*Nods. Stands.*) I hope I've done the right thing at last.

WATSON. You have.

MRS. BARRYMORE. If you have no more questions—

WATSON. Later, perhaps.

(*She moves Up Center, turns to look at the portrait.*)

SIR HENRY. What is it?

MRS. BARRYMORE. I was thinking how the evil legacy of Sir Hugo hangs on. It would have been better if he'd never been born. (*She nods, Exits Up Center.*)

WATSON. Little late to worry about that. (*The letter.*) What do you make of this? L.L.

SIR HENRY. Laura Lyons.

WATSON. Old Frankland's daughter? Of course!

SIR HENRY. (*Looks to doors.*) There is someone out there!

WATSON. Outside the house?

SIR HENRY. Yes. (*Quick,* SIR HENRY *moves to the fireplace and seizes a poker.*)

WATSON. No need for that, Sir Henry. I have a revolver. (WATSON *dips into his pocket and produces a small pistol. Both move for the French doors. A shape materializes outside the room, quickly opens the French doors, slips inside with force and assurance—* SHERLOCK HOLMES.)

HOLMES. No need for weaponry, gentlemen. Your intruder is an ally.

WATSON. Holmes!

SIR HENRY. We thought you were in London.

HOLMES. Which is exactly what I wanted you to think. (SIR HENRY *returns the poker to the fireplace, stands Stage Right.*) I think you'd be more comfortable seated, Watson. I'd appreciate it if you'd point that revolver in another direction. (WATSON *pockets the gun, sits on the sofa.*)

SIR HENRY. I never was more glad to see anyone in my life.

WATSON. Where have you been?

HOLMES. On the moor.

WATSON. Since when?

HOLMES. Since the day Lady Agatha invited us for tea.

SIR HENRY. Then you've never left?

HOLMES. That is correct.

WATSON. (*Pouts.*) You might have trusted me to keep your confidence.

HOLMES. My dear fellow, you have been invaluable to me in this as in many other cases. In your kindness you might have brought me out some comfort or other, and an unnecessary risk would be run.

WATSON. You underestimate me, Holmes.

HOLMES. Never. I know, my dear Watson, that you share my love of all that is bizarre and outside the conventions and humdrum of everyday life. I trust you've kept notes, jotted everything down.

WATSON. I have.

HOLMES. Splendid.

WATSON. I still don't see the need for your deception.

HOLMES. Had I remained with you and Sir Henry my point of view would have been the same as yours. My presence would have warned the menace to be on its guard. In one disguise or another I have moved about freely.

SIR HENRY. What did you learn on the moor?

HOLMES. Considerable.

WATSON. That doesn't tell us much.

SIR HENRY. What's after me? Human or supernatural? Flesh and blood, or the devil?

HOLMES. For the time being I'm afraid I will have to hold that question in abeyance.

SIR HENRY. Why do you avoid answering me?

HOLMES. In a modest way I have combated evil, but to take on the Father of Evil himself would, perhaps, be too ambitious a task. (*Quick, precise, professional.*) Now, Sir Henry, did you see anyone in this room earlier? In the dark?

SIR HENRY. Yes.

HOLMES. Who?

SIR HENRY. Barrymore.

HOLMES. You mean *Mrs.* Barrymore, don't you?

SIR HENRY. No. It was Barrymore.

HOLMES. Sir Henry, have you been conscious of a "presence" somewhere in the house from time to time?

SIR HENRY. I have.

WATSON. The place has an eerie quality about it. Perfectly natural reaction.

HOLMES. I think I can prove you wrong, Watson. Did Barrymore have a flashlight with him?

SIR HENRY. I'm sure he didn't.

HOLMES. Did you disturb him when you entered the room?

SIR HENRY. I think I did.

(WATSON *and* SIR HENRY *exchange a perplexed glance.*
HOLMES *looks from corner to corner. His eyes hit
the desk.*)

HOLMES. Ah, the desk! The perfect hiding place for the unimaginative mind taken unaware.

SIR HENRY. Mr. Holmes, I know the contents of that desk. There's no flashlight there.

HOLMES. (*He marches to the desk, goes through a drawer and, then, another.*) It is a capital mistake,

Sir Henry, to theorize before you have all the evidence. (*He pulls out the flashlight.*) Eureka!

WATSON. So Barrymore had a flashlight. What does that signify?

HOLMES. I expected better of you, Watson. Think, man.

SIR HENRY. You mean he was searching for something in the room. In the dark. He didn't want to be discovered.

HOLMES. No, Sir Henry, what he was after was not in this room. (*Points.*) It was out there. On the moor. (*Rush of Wind.*) Watson, the lights. (WATSON *stands, moves to Dim the Lighting. Again, the room is cloistered in eerie shadows.*) Come close, Sir Henry. I shall now demonstrate that my time on the moor was put to good use. (SIR HENRY *moves behind* HOLMES *at French doors;* WATSON *follows.*) Keep your eyes focused on the near clump of rocks.

WATSON. How can we? The mist has blocked out everything.

HOLMES. Not quite. (*He repeats the business* BARRYMORE *did earlier. He snaps the flashlight on and off . . . on and off . . . on and off . . .*)

WATSON. What are you doing?

HOLMES. I should think that's fairly obvious.

SIR HENRY. You're signaling someone.

WATSON. Who?

HOLMES. That is only one part of the puzzle.

SIR HENRY. Look! There's a light out there.

WATSON. They're answering your signal, Holmes.

HOLMES. No, Watson, not my signal.

SIR HENRY. (*Angry,* SIR HENRY *storms back to the fireplace, picks up the poker.*) I've had enough of it. Who or whatever is out there means to do me harm. I intend to put a stop to it. (*He takes a step in.* HOLMES *moves Center to stop him.*)

HOLMES. No, Sir Henry. That is precisely what they

wish you to do. Remember my warning—you must not venture onto the moor at night.

SIR HENRY. What's out there, Mr. Holmes? You know, don't you?

HOLMES. There is more evil surrounding Baskerville Hall than I have ever encountered before.

(Sound of "Something" on the moor—vague, distant.)

WATSON. Listen!

SIR HENRY. It can't be—

HOLMES. I fear it is. The horror that killed Sir Charles is prowling the moor once again.

(SIR HENRY stands motionless, terrified. WATSON, in fear and wondering, continues to stare out into the mist. Again, the Howl of the Hound—louder and more chilling than before, like a cursed soul that can find no rest. What's left of the room's Stage Lighting Dims quickly, leaving the trio in near silhouette. Another Howl . . .)

CURTAIN—END OF ACT ONE

ACT TWO

Scene 1

At Rise: *Two days later.* Mrs. Barrymore *is showing in* Laura Lyons. *She's a poised, direct, capable young woman.*

Mrs. Barrymore. If you'll come in here, my dear, and wait. (*She indicates the sofa.* Laura *Crosses to it, sits.*) I'll tell Mr. Holmes you're here.

Laura. You might also tell him my time is as valuable as his. I would prefer not to be kept waiting.

Mrs. Barrymore. (*She is taken aback by the severity of* Laura's *tone.*) I'll tell him. (*She Exits Up Center, turns Left.* Laura *sits a moment, impatient. Looks at the portrait, stands, moves to it, studies Sir Hugo's visage.*)

Jack. (*He Enters via the French doors.*) I saw you driving by the cottage. I thought you might stop in.

Laura. (*Turns.*) I planned to on my way back.

Jack. You really shouldn't take that old car of yours on these dirt roads. They're fit for nothing but pony carts.

Laura. I wouldn't do it at night.

Jack. You could skid into the mire.

Laura. You do worry about me, don't you?

Jack. When you let me.

Laura. You must be on good terms with Sir Henry.

Jack. What makes you think that?

Laura. The way you walk into his home.

Jack. The moor is free and easy about such things.

Laura. Nothing's easy on the moor, Jack.

Jack. (*Moves behind Down Left Center chair.*) Come to pay your respects to Sir Henry?

Laura. Why should I? I'm no longer a neighbor of Baskerville Hall.

41

JACK. Then why are you here?

HOLMES. (*He Enters Up Center, from Left.*) Perhaps I can answer that, Mr. Stapleton. I called Mrs. Lyons and asked for this meeting. (*To* LAURA.) There was no need to trouble yourself. I planned to see you in Tracey Coombes.

LAURA. I'll be spending some time with a friend, so I thought I would save you the trouble.

HOLMES. A friend here on the moor, you mean?

LAURA. Lady Agatha.

HOLMES. My associate, Doctor Watson, is at her cottage now. I had no idea she was that social.

LAURA. Perhaps, I should have made an appointment.

HOLMES. Not at all. Your arrival is most opportune. (*To* JACK.) Sorry I haven't taken you up on your invitation to view your insect collection, Stapleton. A situation I hope to remedy.

JACK. You'll find my collection quite special.

HOLMES. Mr. Stapleton and I met on the moor not long ago. He was in pursuit of a Grizzled Skipper butterfly.

JACK. It escaped my net.

HOLMES. Pity. Are you waiting to see Sir Henry?

JACK. My sister and I, yes.

HOLMES. Might try the potting shed. He and Barrymore were there earlier.

JACK. Will you give me a ride back when you leave?

LAURA. Happy to.

JACK. I have only a few things to say to Sir Henry. I won't be long. (*He Exits Left.*)

HOLMES. Old friends?

LAURA. Mr. Stapleton has been exceedingly . . . helpful.

HOLMES. Won't you sit down?

LAURA. (*She returns to the sofa.*) There's a great deal of excitement in the village.

HOLMES. (*Moves Down Center.*) Oh?

LAURA. The police have traced a dangerous convict

to the moor. Apparently, he escaped from Princetown prison sometime ago.

HOLMES. That would be Selden, the Notting Hill murderer.

LAURA. You're well informed, Mr. Holmes.

HOLMES. In some circles there's considerable doubt as to his sanity.

LAURA. Sane or insane, the farmers here about don't like it.

HOLMES. I understand they get a hundred pounds if they can give information.

LAURA. The chance of a hundred pounds is a poor thing compared to the chance of having your throat cut. Surely, we're not to discuss a convict who may or may not be insane.

HOLMES. I understand you had the pleasure of knowing Sir Charles.

LAURA. (She cools. She doesn't care for the drift of the conversation.) Yes.

HOLMES. And I've had the pleasure of knowing your father.

LAURA. I don't know what you're driving at, Mr. Holmes. There is nothing in common between my father and me. I owe him nothing, and his friends are not mine. If it were not for Sir Charles and some other kind hearts I might have starved for all that my father cared.

HOLMES. Did you correspond with Sir Charles?

LAURA. Why are you asking these questions?

HOLMES. I assure you, Mrs. Lyons, they are necessary.

LAURA. (Gives in.) I wrote to him once or twice to thank him for his kindness.

HOLMES. Kindness? Would you care to explain?

LAURA. I've already explained as much. He contributed money so I could set up a small shop in Tracey Coombes.

HOLMES. Have you the dates of those letters?

LAURA. Dates? No.

HOLMES. Did you ever write to Sir Charles asking him to meet you?

LAURA. (*Nervous.*) That's an odd question.

HOLMES. I intend to repeat it. (*Insists.*) Did you ever write to Sir Charles asking him to meet you?

LAURA. No.

HOLMES. Not on the day of his death?

LAURA. No.

HOLMES. Surely your memory deceives. I could even quote a passage of your communication. It ran, "Please, please, as you are a gentleman burn this letter, and be at the gate by ten o'clock."

LAURA. Then he didn't do as I asked.

HOLMES. You do Sir Charles an injustice. He did burn the letter. Most of it, in any case.

LAURA. All right. I wrote it. I wished him to assist me further. I thought that if I had an interview I could gain his help, so I asked him to meet me.

HOLMES. At an hour when the moor is deserted and dark.

LAURA. The hour seemed unimportant.

HOLMES. You asked him to meet you *outside* the house.

LAURA. What does it matter? I never went.

HOLMES. Why?

LAURA. A private matter. It concerns only me.

HOLMES. Why deny you wrote the letter?

LAURA. Obvious, I should think. Gossip.

HOLMES. You admit you made an appointment with Sir Charles at the hour and place he met his death.

LAURA. I do.

HOLMES. Yet you deny you kept the appointment.

LAURA. Yes. (*She sits like a block of ice.*)

HOLMES. Is that all you wish to tell me?

LAURA. Mr. Holmes, that is all I am going to tell you. (*She stands.*) I'll wait for Mr. Stapleton in the car. (*She Exits Up Center, turns Right.*)

HOLMES. (*To himself.*) Remarkable woman. Not to the manner born, but giving an excellent imitation. (*Sniffs.*)

KATHY. (*She Enters via the French doors, watches.*) You're a bloodhound in the true sense of the word, Mr. Holmes.

HOLMES. There are seventy-five perfumes, which it is very necessary that a criminal expert be able to distinguish from each other. Mrs. Lyons favors none of them.

KATHY. (*Moves into the room.*) How did you find her?

HOLMES. I didn't. She found me. I must say she isn't quite what I expected.

KATHY. What did you expect?

HOLMES. Someone less sure of herself.

SIR HENRY. (*He Enters Up Center carrying a shoe. To* KATHY.) I saw you walking over the moor from my window.

KATHY. It's Jack. He has something to say. He went looking for you.

HOLMES. I'm afraid I misdirected him to the potting shed.

KATHY. (*She moves to the French doors, calls out.*) Jack! (*To others.*) He's already on his way back.

HOLMES. The shoe doesn't fit properly?

SIR HENRY. It fits, but there's only one.

HOLMES. Where is its companion?

SIR HENRY. Haven't the slightest idea. (*He puts it on the floor, by the sofa.*)

JACK. (*He Enters Left, stands awkwardly.*) I should have returned long before this, Sir Henry.

SIR HENRY. (*Distant.*) You have something to say to me?

JACK. I do. (*He looks at* HOLMES.) It's rather personal.

SIR HENRY. Anything you have to say to me, you may say in front of Mr. Holmes.

HOLMES. My presence isn't required.

JACK. Thank you, Mr. Holmes. And you will come and see my collection. I'm anxious for your reaction.

HOLMES. You may count on it. (HOLMES *Exits Up Center, turns Left.*)

KATHY. My brother wants to apologize for his temper.

JACK. (*He turns on her, his words harsh, biting.*) I prefer to speak for myself!

KATHY. (*Cowed.*) I didn't mean to speak for you, Jack.

JACK. Then don't. (*Softer tone to* SIR HENRY.) You must understand the thought of losing my sister was hard for me. She's all I have for family. I suspected your motives, that you were simply using your title and position to impress her.

SIR HENRY. Nothing could have been further from my intent.

JACK. I know that—now.

SIR HENRY. I must tell you, Stapleton, that I have every intention of marrying your sister. She's told you?

JACK. She has. I will withdraw all opposition if you promise to wait three months until you are completely sure that marriage is what you truly want. I've seen one unhappy marriage on the moor. I've no desire to see another. My sister's happiness is my only concern.

SIR HENRY. Kathy is no Laura Lyons and I'm no idle painter of pastoral scenes.

JACK. Then we are agreed? Three months?

SIR HENRY. (*Nods assent.*) What must be must be. Three months. (JACK *extends his hand. They shake.*)

KATHY. Wonderful.

JACK. Will you be riding back with Laura and me, Kathy?

KATHY. I'll walk back.

JACK. I'm not sure that's wise. That convict might be lurking.

SIR HENRY. I'll see that Kathy gets home without incident.

JACK. Thank you, Sir Henry. I wonder—would you dine with us at the cottage tomorrow evening?

SIR HENRY. Delighted.

JACK. I'll go find Laura. (*He Exits via the French doors.* KATHY *moves to* SIR HENRY, *elated.*)

SIR HENRY. I'm not so sure I like that provision of three months. If it will make things easier with your brother, I'm not going to argue.

KATHY. I knew he'd come around.

SIR HENRY. (*Sits Down Left Center.*) Kathy, have you always been afraid of your brother?

KATHY. Yes, I think I have.

SIR HENRY. He's never harmed you in any way?

KATHY. (*Avoids the question.*) I was surprised to find Laura was here.

SIR HENRY. So was Mr. Holmes, I think.

PERKINS. (*She Enters Up Center.*) Mrs. Barrymore said you were looking for me, sir.

SIR HENRY. (*Points to the shoe.*) I can't find my other shoe.

PERKINS. (*Crosses, picks it up.*) Aren't these the shoes you gave me yesterday for polish?

SIR HENRY. Barrymore brought them back to my room last night. When I went to put them on just now, I could find only one.

PERKINS. I can't imagine where the other one is, sir.

SIR HENRY. My favorite pair.

PERKINS. I'll turn the place upside down.

SIR HENRY. No need to do that. Just see if you can locate the mate.

PERKINS. I'll try, Sir Henry. I can't imagine what's become of it. Will you be staying for tea, Miss?

KATHY. (*Grins.*) If Sir Henry has no objection.

SIR HENRY. You'll be seeing a great deal of Miss Stapleton around Baskerville Hall in the coming weeks, Perkins.

PERKINS. That will be nice, sir. Especially if the Barrymores leave. I wouldn't like being the only woman here. I scare easily. (*She Exits Up Center, turns Right.*)

KATHY. Are they really leaving?

SIR HENRY. Not immediately. Can't say I blame them. Kathy, you do understand the danger? The curse of the Baskervilles. Oh, I try to pretend everything is perfectly normal, and act according but I know there's a sword hanging over my head, ready to drop at any minute.

KATHY. Henry, whatever this thing is, we'll defeat it together. Mr. Holmes will let no harm come to you. You've got to believe that.

SIR HENRY. I try.

KATHY. I'll see if I can't arrange a nice bouquet for the tray. The wildflowers are almost done for this time of the year.

SIR HENRY. Don't be long. (KATHY *Exits Left, onto the moor, almost colliding with* BARRYMORE.)

BARRYMORE. I beg your pardon, Miss Stapleton.

KATHY. No harm done.

BARRYMORE. (*He waits until* KATHY *is outside, then Enters.*) I've taken an inventory of everything in the potting shed, Sir Henry. You'll be needing some new tools.

SIR HENRY. You haven't been entirely honest with me, have you, Barrymore? (*Moves Down Left.*)

BARRYMORE. About the inventory?

SIR HENRY. No.

BARRYMORE. I'm afraid I don't understand, sir.

SIR HENRY. Your family has lived with mine for generations under this roof, and here I find you in some dark plot against me.

BARRYMORE. I assure you, Sir Henry, you have no reason to think such a thing.

SIR HENRY. Haven't I?

MRS. BARRYMORE. (*She Enters Up Center, from*

Right.) Beg pardon, Sir Henry, Perkins says there's something amiss with one of your shoes. (*She senses the tension in the room, looks to her husband.*) What's wrong?

BARRYMORE. Sir Henry believes I engage in some dark plot against him.

SIR HENRY. I'm not fooled by your tricks with the flashlight at the window. (MRS. BARRYMORE *is startled, suppresses a gasp.*) Sit down, Mrs. Barrymore. You look unwell.

MRS. BARRYMORE. (*Moves to sofa, sits.*) No, no, sir. You misunderstand. No plot against you.

SIR HENRY. (*He stands, moves Up Center, calls off.*) Mr. Holmes! Mr. Holmes! (*He turns back, steps Center.*)

BARRYMORE. (*To his wife.*) We have to go. This is the end of it. You can pack our things.

MRS. BARRYMORE. I've brought us to this. It's my doing, Sir Henry. All mine. My husband has done nothing except for my sake and because I asked him.

SIR HENRY. What does that mean?

BARRYMORE. My wife is speaking the truth. If there was a plot it was not against you.

MRS. BARRYMORE. My unhappy brother is starving on the moor.

BARRYMORE. We couldn't let him perish. (HOLMES *Enters Up Center from Left.*)

SIR HENRY. You mean your brother is—

BARRYMORE. The escaped convict, sir.

HOLMES. (*Annoyed.*) Sir Henry, I expressly asked that you leave this matter to me. I told you you had nothing to fear from the light on the moor.

SIR HENRY. I think, Mr. Holmes, it's time I took a hand in all this.

HOLMES. That would be a most unwise maneuver.

MRS. BARRYMORE. Selden is my younger brother. We humored him when he was a lad and gave him his own way in everything. When he grew older he fell in with a bad lot, the devil was in him. From crime to crime he sank lower and lower.

BARRYMORE. He's quite mad.

MRS. BARRYMORE. Don't say that.

BARRYMORE. He came here for help.

MRS. BARRYMORE. Dragged himself here one night, starving. I couldn't refuse to help him.

SIR HENRY. Haven't you overstepped yourself, Mr. Holmes? Selden is a wanted criminal. Dangerous.

HOLMES. I assure you, Sir Henry, Selden is dangerous to no one but himself. His mind most certainly is deranged, but in a childlike manner. He is not the same man as when he murdered. My guess would be drug damage. I've seen cases like his before. Selden will end his days as little more than a vegetable—passive, frightened, disoriented. (MRS. BARRYMORE *cries, takes out a handkerchief.*) No harm will come to him, Mrs. Barrymore. If he's in danger of apprehension I have instructed him to come immediately to Baskerville Hall.

BARRYMORE. You've talked to him?

HOLMES. He has been on the moor for some weeks, and he has proved invaluable to me, a fact I shall relay to the authorities. (PERKINS *Enters Up Center holding an envelope.*)

SIR HENRY. What is it, Perkins?

PERKINS. I found this under the door, sir. In the kitchen. I heard someone outside, but when I looked I couldn't see anyone.

SIR HENRY. Let me have it.

HOLMES. One moment, Sir Henry. Are you in the custom of receiving mail in this manner?

SIR HENRY. Under the kitchen door? Certainly not.

HOLMES. Give me the letter, Perkins. (*She looks to* SIR HENRY, *he nods.* PERKINS *hands the letter to* HOLMES. *He takes it and moves, Down to the desk, picks up a magnifying glass. All watch.*) Curious.

SIR HENRY. What is it?

HOLMES. Unless I'm mistaken this is the same stationery used for your London warning. (HOLMES *opens the letter.*)

SIR HENRY. What . . . what's the message?

HOLMES. (*Reads.*) "If you value your life, leave Baskerville Hall tonight. There'll be no further warning."

SIR HENRY. The words clipped from a newspaper and stuck to the page?

HOLMES. Not this time. It's handwritten and it's signed. (*All tense.*)

MRS. BARRYMORE. Signed?

HOLMES. Signed . . . Lady Agatha Mortimer. (*The Others exchange astonished looks with one another.* HOLMES *studies the page with the magnifying glass.*) Interesting.

CURTAIN

ACT TWO

SCENE 2

AT RISE: *That evening. The mist is on the moor and, once again, the lighting in the room causes shadows and an atmosphere of foreboding.* HOLMES *is standing in front of the portrait. Voices Up Center, from Right.*

WATSON'S VOICE. We'll soon discover the mystery, Lady Agatha.

LADY AGATHA'S VOICE. I trust so. It's a nuisance being called away at this hour.

WATSON. (*He and* LADY AGATHA *Enter Up Center.*) There you are, Holmes.

HOLMES. (*Turns.*) I see Barrymore reached you. Good of you to come, Lady Agatha.

LADY AGATHA. (*She Crosses Down, sits Down Left Center.*) He said it was urgent.

HOLMES. It is.

WATSON. Dash it, Holmes, we hadn't even sat down to dinner.

HOLMES. My apologies.

WATSON. I'm famished.

HOLMES. You make too much of food, Watson. You should follow my example. I am perfectly content with a roast beef sandwich and a cryptogram.

WATSON. Unfortunately, I can't eat cryptograms. Besides, it wasn't a roast beef sandwich. It was steak and kidney pie. My favorite. Lady Agatha was expecting a guest, too. I was looking forward to company.

HOLMES. Laura Lyons.

LADY AGATHA. She hadn't arrived by the time Barrymore called.

HOLMES. Odd. She left Baskerville Hall some hours ago.

LADY AGATHA. Not alone? They suspect that escaped convict is still on the moor.

HOLMES. Stapleton was with her.

LADY AGATHA. He knows the moor as well as anyone.

WATSON. No one knows this area as well as you, Lady Agatha.

LADY AGATHA. You've discovered something of importance, haven't you, Mr. Holmes? That's why you sent Barrymore.

WATSON. Holmes, I think your holiday to this part of the country was carefully planned. I don't think you were interested in those smelly old huts at all. I think you were only interested in Baskerville Hall.

HOLMES. (*He Crosses behind the sofa, hands the letter to* WATSON, *indicates* LADY AGATHA.) Watson, if you'd be so kind. (*He takes the letter and hands it to* LADY AGATHA.)

LADY AGATHA. (*Reads, then:*) Outrageous.

HOLMES. I take it you disown authorship?

LADY AGATHA. "If you value your life, leave Baskerville Hall tonight. There'll be no further warning." Why, whoever signed my name hasn't the remotest idea of my handwriting style.

HOLMES. I suspected as much. Are you familiar with your guest's handwriting?

LADY AGATHA. Watson here has a bold hand.

HOLMES. I wasn't referring to Doctor Watson. I meant Laura Lyons.

LADY AGATHA. I am quite familiar with her penmanship. (*Positive.*) Laura did not write this message.

WATSON. Why would anyone sign Lady Agatha's name, and not even make an attempt at a good forgery?

HOLMES. To delay investigation, possibly. I don't think the signature is important. The writer was intent in pressing the warning. The net draws tighter.

WATSON. It settles one issue.

HOLMES. Which is?

WATSON. There's no supernatural force behind this ugly business.

HOLMES. Then how do you account for the beast you described to me—dripping with a bluish flame, eyes ringed with fire?

WATSON. (*Frowns.*) I'd forgotten about him.

HOLMES. I haven't.

LADY AGATHA. The moor plays tricks, Doctor Watson. You saw something you mistook for the spectre.

WATSON. You've certainly changed your tune. I know what I saw.

HOLMES. In that case are we to surmise your spectral beast can also weild pen and ink?

WATSON. You're being rude, Holmes. (WATSON *is offended, moves to the desk, sits.*)

HOLMES. No need to take offense.

WATSON. (*Still pouting, sotto.*) Positively rude.

LADY AGATHA. I take it you have suspicions about Laura?

HOLMES. Suspicions about many things. Were you aware she was in correspondence with Sir Charles?

LADY AGATHA. No.

HOLMES. Were you aware that Barrymore was in London the exact time Sir Henry received the first warning.

LADY AGATHA. Barrymore never leaves the moor.

HOLMES. You are mistaken. I have it on authority that he left Baskerville Hall during Sir Henry's London stay.

WATSON. What authority?

HOLMES. A gentleman on the moor.

WATSON. You mean Jack Stapleton?

LADY AGATHA. You'll be casting your doubts on me next, Mr. Holmes. (*Stands.*) You don't think I had a hand in this?

HOLMES. You did leave out one extremely revealing fact when you first called upon my assistance.

LADY AGATHA. I told you everything.

HOLMES. Everything?

LADY AGATHA. I'm not in the habit of lying.

HOLMES. You neglected to mention one salient point. You are executrix of Sir Charles' estate.

LADY AGATHA. (*She stiffens, calmly—*) What if I am?

HOLMES. In the event any misfortune should befall Sir Henry, who has yet to make a will, you would be in a most enviable situation.

WATSON. You go too far, Holmes.

HOLMES. On the contrary. I don't go far enough.

LADY AGATHA. Not telling you was an oversight on my part, nothing more.

HOLMES. Indeed.

LADY AGATHA. You know of my bad financial situation.

HOLMES. Thanks to Watson here.

LADY AGATHA. (*Turns to* WATSON.) He always did have a *rather large mouth.*

WATSON. (*Livid.*) I protest.

(*Sound of the Hound—distant, vague.*)

HOLMES. Quiet.

PERKINS. (*She Enters Up Center, from Right.*) Mr. Holmes, have you seen Sir Henry about?

HOLMES. Ssssssh!

(PERKINS *stands motionless. No one moves—then— the Howl of the Hound—loud, incessant, blood- chilling.*)

LADY AGATHA. It's close to the house.

HOLMES. (*To* PERKINS.) What about Sir Henry?

PERKINS. He's not in his room.

WATSON. Where could he have got to?

HOLMES. The hound! Come, Watson! We may be too late! (*He moves fast to the French doors, opens them, Exits into the night,* WATSON *right behind him.*)

PERKINS. (*Alarmed.*) What is it? What's wrong?

LADY AGATHA. Get Barrymore.

PERKINS. Barrymore?

LADY AGATHA. Stop asking so many questions. Do as you're told. Be quick about it.

PERKINS. Yes, m'am. (*She runs out.*)

(LADY AGATHA *moves to the French doors, looks out. Howl of the Hound again. Worried, She backs into the room. She looks at the letter in her hand, thinks. She moves to the fireplace, takes a match- box from the mantle and prepares to burn the letter as, quickly,* MRS. BARRYMORE *Enters.*)

MRS. BARRYMORE. Perkins whimpered something about the hound and Sir Henry. (*Sees* LADY AGATHA.) What are you doing?

LADY AGATHA. (*Pockets the letter, lies.*) I was going to light the fire. It's not important now. We need your husband. Where is he?

MRS. BARRYMORE. Perkins is fetching him. (*Looks about the empty room.*) Where are Mr. Holmes and Doctor Watson?

LADY AGATHA. (*She moves behind sofa.*) They've gone onto the moor.

MRS. BARRYMORE. (*Distraught, fearing for her brother.*) They're not going to do him any harm? (*Moves to French doors.*) Mr. Holmes promised to protect him.

LADY AGATHA. Who are you talking about?

MRS. BARRYMORE. He's like a child now. He wouldn't hurt anyone.

(BARRYMORE *Enters Up Center, hurriedly.*)

LADY AGATHA. They'll need help, Barrymore . . . Mr. Holmes. Watson. They've gone after Sir Henry. He's out there.

BARRYMORE. Sir Henry never goes on the moor at night.

LADY AGATHA. Don't waste time.

MRS. BARRYMORE. Get the strong light. In the hall chest. (*He Exits Up Center.*) They mustn't harm him.

LADY AGATHA. Why should they want to do harm to Sir Henry? You don't talk sense, woman.

MRS. BARRYMORE. Not Sir Henry. My brother. He's been out there for weeks.

LADY AGATHA. Brother?

MRS. BARRYMORE. (*Moves back into room.*) Selden, the Notting Hill murderer.

LADY AGATHA. The escaped convict who has the countryside terrified?

MRS. BARRYMORE. Yes.

LADY AGATHA. (*Aghast.*) You've known he's been out there? And you've said nothing!

MRS. BARRYMORE. Mister Holmes said he would help him.

LADY AGATHA. It isn't your brother they went after. It's the hound.

MRS. BARRYMORE. (*She, emotionally exhausted, sits Down Left Center.*) This place is cursed. I never wanted to believe that, but it's true.

LADY AGATHA. Stop talking rubbish. I'd better see if there's need for me.

MRS. BARRYMORE. No, don't leave me.

LADY AGATHA. I'll get a sedative for you.

BARRYMORE. (*He Enters holding the flashlight. He holds it up.*) It has a good beam to cut the fog.

WATSON. (*He Enters via French doors. He looks exhausted, defeated.*) I'm afraid that will be of no help.

LADY AGATHA. (*Wary.*) Sir Henry?

WATSON. (*A pause, then:*) Dead.

(*General reaction. WATSON moves Down to the desk, pours himself a drink from a decanter.*)

LADY AGATHA. Impossible!

(*Barrymores are struck dumb. Positions at this point as follows: WATSON at the desk, MRS. BARRYMORE in the chair Down Left Center. BARRYMORE Up Center., LADY AGATHA in front of sofa.*)

WATSON. If that were only true. (*Grim.*) I've never heard screams like that from any man or woman. (*LADY AGATHA sits on sofa, numb.*) The beast had bitten and clawed and chewed.

MRS. BARRYMORE. Doctor Watson, please.

WATSON. You'll have to excuse my nerves. I've never encountered anything like this before. The supernatural is quite beyond me.

BARRYMORE. What could have possessed him to go onto the moor after all the warnings?

WATSON. I don't know. He tried to flee, but the creature was too swift.

LADY AGATHA. Uncle and nephew—murdered. One frightened to death by the sight of the beast.

WATSON. The other driven to his end in his flight to escape from it. I'll be along in a moment. Give him a hand will you, Barrymore?

LADY AGATHA. Better bring the body in here.

HOLMES. (*He Enters, cold, precise, efficient.*) That won't be necessary.

LADY AGATHA. There can be no mistake? He's dead.

HOLMES. There is no mistake.

MRS. BARRYMORE. Poor, poor Sir Henry.

HOLMES. I'm afraid your sympathy is misplaced. You will have to prepare yourself for another shock.

BARRYMORE. How do you mean, sir?

HOLMES. In his distress, Watson neglected to wait for my complete report. True, the man is dead. But he is a man with a beard.

MRS. BARRYMORE. Beard?

HOLMES. I regret having to bring you this information.

MRS. BARRYMORE. My brother, isn't it?

HOLMES. Yes.

WATSON. Why would the hound attack Seldon?

HOLMES. He attacked a scent. Selden was wearing one of Sir Henry's hunting jackets.

BARRYMORE. I can explain. A woman from the church committee asked if we had anything we might donate for a bazaar. Sir Henry gave some of his old clothes, among other things.

MRS. BARRYMORE. They were warm and comfortable. I thought—why should others have them, when my brother was cold and in rags on the moor.

HOLMES. You have no need to reproach yourself.

MRS. BARRYMORE. (*Fatalistic.*) Perhaps it's for the best. I only wish he didn't die so horribly.

SIR HENRY. (*He Enters Up Center.*) Perkins found me. Said I was wanted.

(*All react.*)

WATSON. Where have you been?

LADY AGATHA. We feared for your life.

WATSON. You promised never to go onto the moor at night.

SIR HENRY. I was in the potting shed. Any prohibition against that, Mister Holmes?

HOLMES. None.

SIR HENRY. Why do you all look so strange?

BARRYMORE. It's my wife's brother, sir. Selden.

WATSON. Savaged by the beast.

SIR HENRY. (*In wonder.*) Then the curse doesn't only concern the Baskervilles.

HOLMES. I wish that were true.

SIR HENRY. What connection does Selden have to me?

MRS. BARRYMORE. He was wearing your hunting jacket, sir.

BARRYMORE. The one you donated to the church sale.

HOLMES. The hound had your scent.

SIR HENRY. How could he get my scent in the first place?

LADA AGATHA. When you deal with the supernatural, ordinary explanations are worthless.

HOLMES. I'm afraid I can't agree.

LADY AGATHA. What choice have you?

HOLMES. An investigator needs facts, not legend or rumors. This has not been a satisfactory case.

SIR HENRY. (*Desperate.*) Can't you promise any help?

HOLMES. I can promise you something far more startling than hope.

SIR HENRY. What?

HOLMES. By tomorrow, Sir Henry, the Curse of the Baskervilles will either be broken. Or—

MRS. BARRYMORE. Or?

LADY AGATHA. Or?

HOLMES. Someone in this room will be dead. (*Lights Fade quickly, as—*)

CURTAIN

ACT TWO

SCENE 3

AT RISE: *The following evening. A Storm is building . . . distant Thunder.* SIR HENRY *is busy at the writing desk.* WATSON *stands by the fireplace which sends out a warming glow.*

SIR HENRY. Makes me feel strange. Sitting here writing all this down.

WATSON. One should always keep his affairs in order, Sir Henry.

SIR HENRY. No argument there. Only I've never been concerned about a will before. My own will, that is.

WATSON. You'll feel better for it.

SIR HENRY. Will I?

WATSON. Count on it. Can't imagine why Holmes went to see Lady Agatha this afternoon. Yesterday, he practically accused her of being implicated.

SIR HENRY. At least we're done with that ghastly business with Selden.

WATSON. You're dining with the Stapletons this evening.

SIR HENRY. Unless Mr. Holmes brings up some new objection. (*The writing.*) Somehow I feel this will is a prelude to my— (*He breaks off, not wanting to say the word "death".*)

WATSON. Trust Holmes.

SIR HENRY. I do intellectually. Emotionally I'm tight as a knot inside.

BARRYMORE. (*He, wearing a raincoat, carrying suitcase and hat, Appears Up Center.*) We are leaving now, sir.

(MRS. BARRYMORE *Appears behind her husband. They step in the room.*)

Sir Henry. (*Stands, moves to them.*) There's nothing I can do to change your minds?

Barrymore. I'm afraid not, Sir Henry. I think it best my wife and I started a new life elsewhere.

Sir Henry. I understand. (*Extends his hand.*) Goodbye, Barrymore, and good luck.

Barrymore. Thank you, Sir Henry.

Sir Henry. (*Shakes hands with* Mrs. Barrymore.) Goodbye, Mrs. Barrymore.

Mrs. Barrymore. (*Nods.*) Sir Henry.

Sir Henry. You will write and let me know how things are going?

Barrymore. Yes, sir. (*To his wife.*) We don't want to miss the train. Goodbye, Doctor Watson.

Watson. Goodbye. Luck to both of you.

(*The* Barrymores *Exit Up Center turn Right.*)

Sir Henry. They'll be all right. They did well by my uncle's will.

Watson. Handsomely. Still, I've never trusted Barrymore. (*Thinks.*) I didn't know there was a train at this hour.

Sir Henry. (*Snaps.*) Train? Train? What does a train matter? (*Calms down.*) Forgive me. I'm . . . I'm tense . . .

Watson. I can well believe it. You've been under a terrible strain, and Holmes is up in his room with his foul-smelling tobacco. He says this is a six pipe case.

Laura. (*She Enters Up Center, from Right.*) I'm sorry to intrude like this. Mrs. Barrymore said I should come right in. I'm Mrs. Lyons. Mr. Frankland's daughter.

Sir Henry. I've heard of you. (Laura *doesn't know how she should take this remark.*) This is Doctor Watson.

Laura. (*Nods.*) Oh, yes. Lady Agatha's comrade. She speaks highly of you.

WATSON. Sorry we didn't meet the other evening. Won't you sit down?

LAURA. (*She Crosses to sofa, sits.*) I must see Mr. Holmes. It's important.

WATSON. I'll get him.

LAURA. Thank you.

(WATSON *Exits Up Center, turns Left.*)

SIR HENRY. Aren't you afraid to cross the moor?

LAURA. I understood they captured the convict.

SIR HENRY. That's true.

LAURA. You mean—the storm?

SIR HENRY. I mean the hound.

LAURA. It isn't the other world that will hurt one, Sir Henry. It's the living.

SIR HENRY. I believe I heard Mr. Holmes say you were from the village of Tracey Coombes.

LAURA. I have a small shop.

SIR HENRY. I have a distant relative living there.

LAURA. I've heard of no Baskervilles in the area.

SIR HENRY. No, the name is Desmond. An elderly clergyman. Could I get you something? I fear I'm understaffed at the moment. The maid leaves before dark and the Barrymores have deserted.

LAURA. I saw the suitcases in their grip.

SIR HENRY. Place won't be the same without them.

LAURA. I want you to know, Sir Henry, that I had the utmost respect for your uncle. He was kind, generous and most thoughtful. His death . . . disturbed me.

HOLMES. (*He Enters Up Right.*) I expected to see you earlier than this, Mrs. Lyons.

LAURA. You knew I'd return?

HOLMES. I hoped you would.

SIR HENRY. You'll probably want privacy.

HOLMES. I think you'd best stay, Sir Henry. What Mrs. Lyons is about to reveal concerns you.

(WATSON *Enters Up Center, stands Left.*)

SIR HENRY. Me?

HOLMES. Your uncle, to be precise.

LAURA. You anticipate.

HOLMES. I am a flawless judge of character, Mrs. Lyons. You did not impress me as the sort of female who could live comfortably with a serious lie.

SIR HENRY. What are you driving at?

LAURA. (HOLMES *looks to her—pointedly.*) It is true I wrote the letter to Sir Charles . . .

HOLMES. On the instigation of another.

(LAURA, *troubled.*)

SIR HENRY. What other?

LAURA. I . . . I . . .

HOLMES. I know what you communicated in our earlier interview, and also what you've withheld in connection with this matter. I regard this case as one of murder and the evidence may implicate not only your friend Jack Stapleton, but his wife as well.

LAURA. (*Stands, startled.*) His wife!

SIR HENRY. Wife? What are you saying?

HOLMES. The person who has passed for his sister is really his wife.

WATSON. I don't believe it.

LAURA. Nor I. He's *not* a married man.

HOLMES. Kathy unwittingly revealed the ruse when she told Watson of the school she and her "brother" ran in the north country. (*Fishes out photograph.*) I made inquiries and one of the employees of the school sent on this photograph. (*Hands it to* SIR HENRY.) Four years ago it was taken. I think you will recognize the couple—Mr. and Mrs. Stapleton. The employee has written the identification on the back.

LAURA. Let me see that. (*She takes it from* SIR HENRY, *turns it over.*) It's true.

HOLMES. Stapleton asked you to write the letter to entice Sir Charles out of the house.

LAURA. (*She nods, still staring at the photograph.*)
He . . . he promised to marry me once my problems
were settled.

SIR HENRY. Now I know why Kathy lives in fear of
her "brother."

WATSON. That's why he went into a rage when he
saw you and Kathy close together. He couldn't control
the instincts of a jealous husband.

LAURA. I swear to you when I wrote the letter I
never dreamed of any harm to the cld gentleman. He
had been a good friend.

HOLMES. I presume the reason Stapleton gave was
that you would receive help from Sir Charles for the
legal expense connected with your divorce.

LAURA. Yes. Jack said he couldn't help because he
himself was penniless.

HOLMES. After you sent the letter he dissuaded you
from keeping the appointment.

LAURA. Yes.

HOLMES. Then you heard nothing until you read
of Sir Charles' death.

LAURA. He said the death was a mysterious one,
and that I should certainly be suspected if the facts
came out. He frightened me into remaining silent.

HOLMES. I think, on the whole, you've had a fortu-
nate escape. You had him in your power and he knew
it, and yet you are alive.

LAURA. I couldn't remain silent any longer.

HOLMES. The line between fear and love is often a
thin one. As you have been honest with me, I shall
be honest with you. You are still in danger.

SIR HENRY. He's likely to hurt Kathy.

HOLMES. Not if everything falls into place. Time is
the essential element. Watson, you will escort Mrs.
Lyons to Lady Agatha's cottage.

LAURA. I can take care of myself.

HOLMES. You heard me, Watson.

WATSON. Come along, my dear. You can trust my

protection. (*He opens the French doors.* LAURA *looks once more at the photograph, returns it to* HOLMES.)

LAURA. I was right, y'know. Nothing's easy on the moor. (*She Exits,* WATSON *follows.*)

SIR HENRY. You must really be worried for her safety?

HOLMES. Hang her safety. I merely want some guarantee she won't warn Stapleton.

SIR HENRY. (*Worried.*) We must help Kathy.

HOLMES. You will do exactly as I instruct.

SIR HENRY. I'm ready.

HOLMES. You will walk to Stapleton Cottage, and enjoy your dinner.

SIR HENRY. You're not serious? I'm not sure I can face Jack Stapleton.

HOLMES. That is precisely what you must do. You will divulge the path you will take on your return. Clear?

SIR HENRY. Where will you be?

HOLMES. Nearby. Leave within the hour. (*He steps into the night.* SIR HENRY *is taken aback by* HOLMES *abrupt departure. He Crosses to the French doors.*)

SIR HENRY. Wait a minute, Mr. Holmes! (*Calls after him.*) Holmes! (*Thunder.* SIR HENRY *reluctantly closes the door. He looks about the room feeling a sense of isolation. He moves Up Center.*) Barrymore! Barrymore! (*Suddenly it dawns that the* BARRYMORES *have departed. He forces a smile.*) Better get hold of myself. They're all gone. (*He takes out the pocket watch, checks the hour.*) Wait one hour. (*He pockets the watch, moves to the desk, sits, picks up a pen, his eyes drift to something atop the desk. He picks it up. It's the manuscript of the legend. He can't resist, picks it up, reads. Thunder.*) "Of the origin of the Hound of the Baskerville there have been many statements . . . know then that in the time of the Great Rebellion . . . this Manor of Baskerville was held by Hugo of that name . . . "

(The Lights Flicker from the storm. From outside the house—that unmistakeable Wail of the accursed— The Hound! SIR HENRY startles alert. He gets up, frozen to the spot, his eyes betraying terror. He listens. Again—the Bay, hair-raising, nerve-shattering, ominous! A pause and, then, the laugh of a woman from Up Center. Bewildered, SIR HENRY turns. A moment passes and then KATHY Enters, Right.)

KATHY. Good evening, Henry.

SIR HENRY. *(Amazed.)* Kathy . . . ?

KATHY. *(She grins, her words are cynical, cold, bloodless.)* Yes. Kathy. Sweet, endearing, innocent.

SIR HENRY. What's wrong with you? I told Holmes I was afraid for your life. He knows you're married to Stapleton.

KATHY. Does he? I'll have to deal with that in time.

SIR HENRY. You . . . *(Getting the picture.)* You and Stapleton plotted all this together!

KATHY. Jack? Don't be a fool. He's weak. Never did a thing that I wasn't right there behind him, pushing, insisting. It was all my idea.

SIR HENRY. I . . . I don't understand . . .

KATHY. He's the son of Rodger Baskerville, the younger brother of Sir Charles, the one who fled to South America and "supposedly" died unmarried. Now everything will be Jack's and that means—mine.

SIR HENRY. *(Devastated.)* He's my cousin . . .

(Another Wail from the Hound. SIR HENRY reacts. KATHY grins.)

KATHY. It's outside the front door. Chained. I waited until the house was empty, 'til the moor was dark.

SIR HENRY. What . . . what is it?

KATHY. You'll soon see. He's starved. I keep him that way. I'm going to release him.

SIR HENRY. No!

KATHY. You have only one chance. Onto the moor, Henry! Run, run, run. Outrace him if you can! It's your only hope! Run!

(*Confused, frantic,* SIR HENRY *moves for the French door. Sound of Gunfire from Off Right.* KATHY *turns to the sound.* HOLMES *Enters from the moor.*)

HOLMES. That would be for the hound, Mrs. Stapleton.

KATHY. (*Wild-eyed.*) What's happened to him!

HOLMES. I suspect the police have killed the doomed animal. I was able to persuade the wardens and others searching for Seldon to remain in the area for one more night.

KATHY. (*Bitter.*) Jack warned you, didn't he?

HOLMES. You weren't quite as sure of him as you thought.

KATHY. You haven't won yet, Mr. Holmes. There's always Grimpen Mire! (*She runs out Up Center, turns Right.*)

SIR HENRY. Kathy!

HOLMES. You needn't worry, Sir Henry. Her melodramatic gesture is wasted. The house is completely surrounded.

SIR HENRY. How did you know she wouldn't be at the cottage?

HOLMES. An able assist from Lady Agatha. Earlier this evening she tracked Kathy to where the hound was secreted in an abandoned mine. Later, when it was dark, she observed Kathy moving not to the cottage, but to this house.

SIR HENRY. Then there really was a hound.

HOLMES. An enormous dog. Gigantic. Part mastiff, part great Dane.

SIR HENRY. But the glow?

HOLMES. Phosphorus. Your missing shoe would supply the scent.

SIR HENRY. And Stapleton did try to save my life?

HOLMES. In his clumsy fashion. Selden told me that Stapleton, too, was off the moor during your London stay. Also he gave himself away with that hand-written warning. I recognized the scrawl as the same found on the catalogue cards he uses for his butterfly collection.

WATSON. (*He comes hurrying in with* LADY AGATHA, *from outside.*) Holmes, the police have stopped everyone on the moor.

HOLMES. A safety precaution. They'll pick up Jack Stapleton at the cottage and— (*Sound of Whistles in distance.*) Kathy has been apprehended judging from those whistles.

WATSON. (*Befuddled.*) Kathy? What's she got to do with it?

SIR HENRY. How could he possibly hope to claim the inheritance?

HOLMES. Any number of ways. He could claim it from South America, establish identity before the British authorities there. Or, he might adopt an elaborate disguise during the short time he needed to be in London. He might hire an accomplice to impersonate him, retaining a claim on some portion of the income.

LADY AGATHA. I was so afraid you suspected me, I thought of burning the warning with my name on it.

HOLMES. Don't worry about that. I am the last and highest court of appeal in detection, and I exonerate you.

WATSON. (*Pouts.*) Bit pompous, Holmes.

SIR HENRY. Kathy had no feeling for me at all.

HOLMES. If it's any consolation, Sir Henry, the most winning woman I ever knew was hanged for poisoning three little children for their insurance money. Come

Watson, no time to waste if we're to catch that late train.

WATSON. Now? This minute?

HOLMES. There was a most interesting message from Mrs. Hudson. A retired officer from the Palace Guard is being blackmailed by some devilishly clever ruse. I suspect an organized ring with connections in Detroit.

WATSON. But my things, my clothes?

HOLMES. Lady Agatha, if you'll be so kind as to see that Perkins packs everything and sends it off to Baker Street.

LADY AGATHA. First thing in the morning.

HOLMES. (*Moves to French doors.*) Come along, Watson. The game is afoot! (*He's Out like a shot.*)

WATSON. (*He moves to follow, sighs.*) The man has no mercy.

(SIR HENRY *picks up the document that relates the legend and tears it in two.* LADY AGATHA *waves goodbye as the Curtains Close.*)

LADY AGATHA. Come back anytime. You're always welcome.

END OF PLAY

PRODUCTION NOTES

ON STAGE: Fireplace Stage Right with mantle, poker, box of matches, chair on each side of fireplace, portrait of Sir Hugo Baskerville above the mantle. Bookshelves or tables Right and Left of Up Center hallway, desk and chair, Down Left, with writing material, decanter and glasses, manuscript of the legend, magnifying glass. Sofa or chaise lounge Down Right Center; fine chair with side-table Down Left Center. Bell rope. Additional dressing as desired: rugs, books, candlesticks, vases, lamps, etc.

ACT ONE

BROUGHT ON: Wallet with letter (Sir Henry), map (Watson), flowers (Kathy), pocket watch in tissue paper (Kathy), butterfly net (Jack), vase (Perkins), flashlight (Barrymore), tray with mug and pitcher of milk (Perkins), charred letter (Mrs. Barrymore), pistol (Watson), *Weekly Journal* magazine (Perkins).

ACT TWO

Shoe (Sir Henry), envelope with letter (Perkins), letter (Holmes), flashlight (Barrymore), raincoats, suitcases (Barrymores), photograph (Holmes).

COSTUMES

Clothing is contemporary, but should, if possible, lean to tweeds, woolens and outfits suited to the open country of the moor. Mrs. Barrymore might wear an apron over a dark dress. Barrymore should wear a white serving jacket or something that establishes him as the butler.

SOUND EFFECTS

Wind, thunder, gunfire, police whistles, HOWL of The Hound.

SUGGESTIONS

More than any other Sherlock Holmes classic, THE HOUND OF THE BASKERVILLES lends itself to modern costuming and setting. Baskerville Hall, the moor, the brooding isolation of the locale all give an aura of "another time." Naturally, if a production wishes to stick to the original Victorian period and has the resources, all that is necessary is to cut the few lines that pin the time as the present. A nice touch is achieved if the pocket watch Kathy presents to Sir Henry can be "musical." The convict Selden who appears briefly can be portrayed by the stage manager. In the original production this "bit" was done by the actor portraying Jack Stapleton. A beard, ragged clothing, etc. were employed. A good old-fashioned thunder sheet is still the best bet for the storm effects of the final scene. Beware of lighting the set too brightly. Baskerville Hall is a place of shadows. Special attention must be paid to the HOWL of the hound. Make certain it's loud—enough to startle. Again, in the original production, an additional speaker was placed in the rear of the theater to give a truly "panasonic sound" to the howling, which gave the impression the beast was prowling the theater darkness.

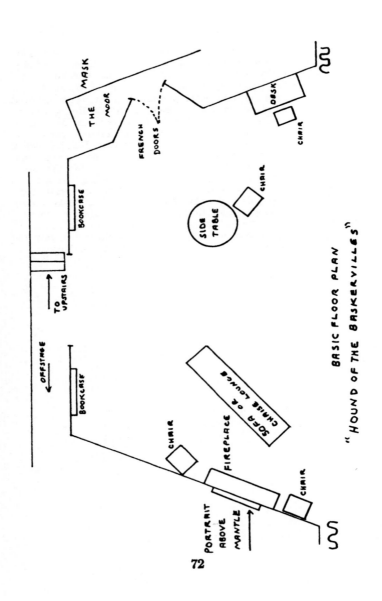

BASIC FLOOR PLAN

"HOUND OF THE BASKERVILLES"

Also By
Tim Kelly

THE BUTLER DID IT

DARK DEEDS AT SWAN'S PLACE (OR NEVER TRUST A TATTOOED SAILOR)

DOG EAT DOG

DON'T BE AFRAID OF THE DARK

EGAD, THE WOMAN IN WHITE (SEALED IN A MAD-HOUSE)

THE FACE ON THE BARROOM FLOOR OR GLIMPSED THOUGH THE SAWDUST

FRANKENSTEIN

THE GIFT AND THE GIVING

HIDE AND SHRIEK

IT WAS A DARK AND STORMY NIGHT

LIFE ON THE BOWERY OF THE LIAR'S DOOM

MURDER IN THE MAGNOLIAS

MY SON IS CRAZY BUT PROMISING

SAY UNCLE, UNCLE SILAS (TRAPPED IN A HOUSE OF FIENDS)

THE SILK SHIRT

THE SOAPY MURDER CASE

THAT'S THE SPIRIT

TRICK OR TREAT

THE ZOMBIE

DANGER- GIRLS WORKING
James Reach

Mystery Comedy / 11f / Unit Set

At a New York girl's boarding house, there is a newspaper woman who wants to write a novel, a wise cracking shop girl, the serious music student, a faded actress, a girl looking for romance, the kid who wants to crash Broadway and other boarders. The landlady, is the proud custodian of the "McCarthy Collection," a group of perfect uncut diamonds. When it disappears from the safe, the newspaper woman is given two hours to solve the case before the police are called. Suspicion is cleverly shifted from one to the other of the girls and there's a very surprising solution.

MURDER AMONG FRIENDS
Bob Barry

Comedy thriller / 4m, 2f / Interior

Take an aging, exceedingly vain actor; his very rich wife; a double dealing, double loving agent, plunk them down in an elegant New York duplex and add dialogue crackling with wit and laughs, and you have the basic elements for an evening of pure, sophisticated entertainment. Angela, the wife and Ted, the agent, are lovers and plan to murder Palmer, the actor, during a contrived robbery on New Year's Eve. But actor and agent are also lovers and have an identical plan to do in the wife. A murder occurs, but not one of the planned ones.

"Clever, amusing, and very surprising."
– *New York Times*

"A slick, sophisticated show that is modern and very funny."
– WABC TV

THE DECORATOR
Donald Churchill

Comedy / 1m, 2f / Interior

Marcia returns to her flat to find it has not been painted as she arranged. A part time painter who is filling in for an ill colleague is just beginning the work when the wife of the man with whom Marcia is having an affair arrives to tell all to Marcia's husband. Marcia hires the painter a part time actor to impersonate her husband at the confrontation. Hilarity is piled upon hilarity as the painter, who takes his acting very seriously, portrays the absent husband. The wronged wife decides that the best revenge is to sleep with Marcia's husband, an ecstatic experience for them both. When Marcia learns that the painter/actor has slept with her rival, she demands the opportunity to show him what really good sex is.

"Irresistible."
– *London Daily Telegraph*

"This play will leave you rolling in the aisles....
I all but fell from my seat laughing."
– *London Star*

Lightning Source UK Ltd.
Milton Keynes UK
UKOW041957170412

190923UK00001B/12/P